Bred by the DRAGON

LYONNE RILEY

Sammy is on her fifth visit to DreamTogether, a breeding program designed to help monsters create the families they've always wanted. But as hard as she and her dragon partner have tried to create a hatchling, every test turns up negative.

Dragons are dying out, so Zakarion came to DreamTogether to continue his species. But when he can no longer sell priceless artifacts from his hoard to pay for his visits, he takes it as a sign to give up.

But Sammy has grown attached to her dragon, and doesn't want to set aside Zakarion's dream. Perhaps dragons aren't meant to breed in sterile medical rooms, so she offers to continue trying to conceive outside of DreamTogether. Given that dragons live centuries while humans don't, Sammy and Zakarion agree to avoid a romantic entanglement—but as they grow closer and closer, that might just prove impossible.

CONTENT WARNINGS

- Stretching and stuffing
- Anonymous sex
- Breeding
- Infertility issues
- Two cocks
- Pregnancy
- Birth

one

SAMMY

"Oh, fuck!" My hands are wrapped around the grips so tight my knuckles are turning white. "Please!"

He knows what I want. We've done this dance before—his upper cock is so big that he likes to tease me with it, just giving me the bumpy, textured crown first, making me hungry and needy.

This is attempt number five. Every month, I come back to DreamTogether, and they strap me face-down to this bench, my feet tucked into stirrups to hold them apart, my legs and arms buckled in. All this fancy equipment? It's here so the big dragon who comes to mate with me doesn't send me sprawling. Rubber coats the underside of the bench, so when he's inside me, he can grip it with his claws and put all his effort into fucking me senseless.

I still don't know his name, but it doesn't matter. Those are the rules. It's all anonymous, and with the way I'm rigged to the bench, I can't see him even if I turn my head. All that's behind me is a red, scaled mass, and sometimes I catch a billow of smoke curling up to the ceiling.

I buck uselessly, trying to push my hips back into his, to take even more of him.

"Nuh uh," he croons in that deep, gravelly voice of his. "You're only going to have what I want to give you."

We've started to learn each other, over time. The dragon wants to make this as pleasurable as possible for me, which he's made perfectly clear by the way he continues to thrust shallowly inside me, just hinting at what else he can give me. I simultaneously love and hate when he taunts me like this, like he's the one in control and I'm there for his use.

Which is, technically, true. And it's hot as hell.

There's no point in begging for more, so I relish what I have, like he told me. He'll take his time, as he always does, even though my body is now well-trained to take his.

Before my first session at DreamTogether, I was provided a dilator to stretch me out. I was more than happy to do it for my new job. Monsters are big, and when I signed up, I checked off the box for every monster possible, excited to see what they could throw at me. That meant I could get a creature as big as a dragon—and sure enough, I did.

The first time he fucked me, it was... a challenge. He had to cover himself and me in lube just to get the head of his giant cock to fit, and damn, it still stretched me as far as I could go. Even now, my pussy is spread as wide as possible to allow him in.

He draws back slightly, almost leaving me, and I whimper in objection. He chuckles behind me and sinks back in, that head covered in little nubs filling me up. Fuck, it feels incredible. This time he pushes deeper, and all my nerve endings are on fire as more of that textured cock slides in. Dragon ladies must be lucky as hell to get fucked like this all the time.

"Your cunt is so good," my dragon groans, still only granting me a few shallow thrusts. And I know he's not just saying that. Sometimes he goes off early, as much as he tries to hold out for me. "So small and so... tight." He pushes in deeper, stimulating more and more of me, more than any human man ever has.

I'm so ruined for humans now.

"Please," I beg again, even though I know it won't get me anywhere. "I need more. Please!"

I can feel his laugh ripple down into his cock. He leans down, his steaming-hot breath tickling the back of my neck, and he buries his snout in my big curls.

"Oh, you want this cock?" he asks, never relenting his slow, purposeful strokes. "You want all of it? Will it fit inside you?"

He knows it will, eventually. This may seem like a taunt, a tease, a slow torture—but he's doing it for a good reason. He doesn't just have girth, but length, as well, and it takes time for me to open up fully for him. The first time we met, he pushed in too deep too soon, and I yelped with pain. Now he takes his time, working me until I'm stretched and waiting for him. Sometimes too much time, like today, when he slips in just a little more, then reels his hips back, leaving only that bumpy crown nestled inside me.

I wish I knew what he looked like. I can see that he has huge, black claws on the tips of his red, scaled fingers. It was strange at first when he wrapped them around the bench, careful not to touch me, but I've gotten used to them. Now, I love when he starts to lose himself in his rutting and grips my hips tight, the tips of his claws stinging as they bite into my ass.

He's not there yet now, though. My dragon is focused on rubbing me with all his built-in nubs, the texture driving me absolutely wild. His second cock hangs lower, but it's still hard and erect, and every time he pushes inside me, the textured nubs on it glance over my clit. Again and again he repeats this torturous motion, and this time he even reaches down with one hand to press that other cock against me as he strokes.

Fuck, I'm a goner.

He's not even halfway inside when my whole body seizes up and I let out a powerful cry. It's not the biggest orgasm he's ever given me, but it's much earlier than usual, and I clench hard around him.

"Oh, damn," he groans, and hot steam hits my back. "You're sensitive today."

"I'm ovulating," I manage between gasps, my body falling limp to the bench. DreamTogether has me track my cycle, and I should be at peak fertility right now.

"Mmm," hums the dragon, his huge hand drawing his claws gently down my back, making me shiver all over. Now that I've loosened a little, he starts moving again, and I'm so overstimulated that I cry out. "You're ripe for my seed, is what you're saying?"

Sometimes he talks like this, as if he's a hundred years old. And, I don't know, maybe he is, or even older. He's a dragon, after all, and while I don't know much about drag- ons, I've read that they live a long time—sometimes up to a millennia.

And there aren't very many of them, so I was surprised when they assigned him to me. He must be one of only a handful left, and in a way I feel... special. Special that I was selected for him to help create the next generation of dragons, special in a way that none of my jobs ever have, like I have a greater purpose.

He likes to make me feel special, too.

"I suppose so," I manage to say as he continues taunting me with his very bountiful cock. "Maybe it will work this—" Suddenly, he plunges in deeper, and I interrupt myself with a cry. "—this time."

As I said, we're on attempt number five. Sometimes it takes a little longer, the clinician assured me. I went through a rather excessive amount of testing before I was even considered for DreamTogether to make sure I had plenty of eggs and I could carry a healthy hybrid baby.

I'm "ripe," as my dragon would say. Very much so.

"It will work," he snarls, thrusting into me again, then withdrawing nearly all the way. "In this perfect, fertile womb? I'll make sure of it."

Now that I've softened up again after my orgasm, he pushes in farther, and my body welcomes him eagerly. The texture of his cock is unreal, and already I'm shivering again. I guess I am more sensitive than usual.

"Your cunt is heavenly," he murmurs, giving a few more experimental pumps of his hips at this depth. I love when he uses words like *cunt*. I sag forward on the bench, and he lets out a guttural moan as he fills me even fuller, asking me to make room for him.

Between sessions at DreamTogether, I keep using my dilator to stay spread enough for him. I'm making good use of it now as he reaches *that* part of his cock—the swell that I can tell lies somewhere two-thirds of the way up. The shape of him is unusual in every way, and the number of times I've wished I could simply turn around and look at it...

Well, it's a lot of times.

"Can you take me?" he asks, and it's not in his dirty voice, but his genuine, curious voice.

"I think so," I manage, right as he pulls out, dragging all those lovely nubs along the inside of me. I jolt, and then he reunites with me again, that gentle swell opening me even wider. "I want it."

He grunts in understanding, and gently, works his cock in even farther. The immense stretch is consuming me, firing off one burst of sensation after another each time he strokes. I don't know how he can possibly fit all that inside me, but then...

He does. After the swell, his cock narrows again, and that's when his hips meet my thighs. I've taken as much as I possibly can, and my pussy desperately clenches, but there's so much, almost too much.

Then he pulls out again, letting me recover for a moment before pressing in a second time. My body accepts it even easier, and he groans as more of his weight rests against mine.

My dragon is so huge that I can peer up and see the underside of his throat as his long neck extends out in front of us. If my arms weren't strapped down to the bench, I would love to touch him, to feel his scales under my fingers as he does this. But I'll have to be satisfied with what I have. We've already crossed a lot of lines by becoming as intimate as we have over the last five sessions. I don't think we were intended to enjoy this as much as we do, for starters.

Except that our bodies fit together, well... perfectly. I've never had a lover like him, who cared so much for my pleasure, who read me as well as he does.

Now that he's buried fully inside me, my dragon's breaths speed up, and he starts thrusting faster. He grips the underside of the bench with his claws, clenching me against his body. He makes me feel so small underneath him, like without this bench he could crush me.

Each pump of his hips, each plunge of him inside me, is pulling louder and louder cries from my throat. I'm helpless as his lower cock rubs my clit, the nubs dragging across it with every single stroke.

Sometimes I wonder what would happen if he used both of them. But that, unfortunately, is not essential to what we're doing here, so it's never come up. Besides, it's not like we spend that long chatting before he fucks me. We're both much too eager for that—and DreamTogether is always listening. Exchanging anything too personal is against the rules.

Still, I bet it would feel great to take his two cocks at once. I've done a few adventurous things before, but never *that*.

"You like this, do you?" the dragon asks, which I know is a rhetorical question. Even the first time we had sex, he made me orgasm twice, which is pretty far beyond how most of my sexual interactions go.

"Yes," I squeeze out between cries. "I love it."

With a satisfied, approving groan, he sinks fully inside me again, and I revel in our togetherness. Damn. If I could have this every day, rather than once a month, I would be a happy, happy woman. But once we've succeeded, we won't see each other again. I carry his hatchling for however many months it takes to gestate, and then I'll give it back to him. After that, we have no further business.

This setup should be ideal for someone like me. I've always drifted from boyfriend to boyfriend, never truly connecting with any of them. It always felt like it was missing something, that deeper understanding I've always craved from a partner.

If there's any situation in which there's no deeper understanding or connection, it's getting anonymously fucked by a monster.

"Oh, hell," my dragon says suddenly, and he swells up inside me. "I'm sorry, I—" He buckles forward and moans as his cock gets fatter and thicker, pushing me even wider for him. He's still thrusting, even as he jettisons one hot stream of come into me after another.

"K-keep g-g-going," I cry out, so close to my peak that I could scream. I hear a determined grunt behind me, and with a massive, wet *squelch* he shoves his cock in again, and again, sending his rather gratuitous amount of come spurting out of me. It runs down my legs, dripping across the bench as he keeps pumping into me. He must be incredibly over-sensitive, because he utters helpless, desperate moans with every single stroke, trying to bring me there. I'm climbing higher and higher as those gorgeous nubs of his rub along my walls, as that swell slips in and out.

And then, I break. The wave that sweeps over me is huge, a shadow dwarfing me, crushing me into the earth. I can't even scream because my voice is trapped, the sheer force of my orgasm making sound impossible.

"Mother of—" he mutters. "H-how do you... how do you feel so *good*?" His claws scratch the underside of the bench as he pumps once more, drawing my orgasm out even further while he roars above me.

And then, there's a massive *crack!* Suddenly I'm pressed against a huge, warm body. My dragon shakes all over, his cock finally coming to a rest, fully encased in me.

"Please," I gasp, because he's holding me so tight, and the heavy bench is applying so much pressure to my stomach, that I'm struggling to breathe in air. "I can't—"

"Damn," he says, abruptly separating us. His cock slips

out of me, and I feel his come gush down my legs. "I broke it again."

This is the second time now he's orgasmed so hard that he tore the bench right out of the concrete.

I don't think management is going to like that very much.

two

ZAKARION

DAMN IT. I'M ALWAYS BREAKING WEAK, PATHETIC HUMAN things. I'm just not designed to fit into the human world, as big as I am. They tried to build these benches with monsters in mind, but not dragons, I don't think.

Attempt number five. I didn't think it would take this long, but in a way... I'm glad it has. Sure, it costs a hell of a lot of money. I'm paying DreamTogether a sizable amount for my woman's wages, but it's worth it for the outcome. Not to mention that the process of trying to impregnate her has been delightful, if I'm being even mildly honest about it.

I do think of her as mine, now. I certainly haven't had this much sex in my life. And even the first time with her, though it was tricky to fit, felt as if... our bodies knew each other. I can understand clearly what hers wants, what it needs, what's too much and what's not enough.

It's good we only meet once a month, because if it were more frequent than that, I might simply run out of seed for how much I pour into her every time.

Gently I set the bench down, trying to fit the broken concrete back into place. I test its balance as I release it, to make sure it won't fall over and hurt her.

I don't know her name, so she's simply become "woman" in my head. We're not supposed to share information, even down to our names, though I've almost told her every time and just barely held it back.

Not that it would be too hard to find me if she wanted to. I'm one of perhaps a few dozen dragons left alive—most of whom are already mated, or are distant cousins of mine. Before finding DreamTogether, I reached out to every other female dragon I could find, looking for a mate of my own. It's a little more clinical than online dating when you're the last remaining members of your species. Each of them understood why I was asking such a forward question.

But no, they were all spoken for.

Now I'm glad I chose DreamTogether, because I think this woman will be the perfect carrier for my hatchling. She's strong, with wide hips, broad shoulders, and an impressive butt. I love to see her dark brown flesh squeezed in my claws, bulging out between them.

They really did pick the perfect one for me.

The question remains if it will work. Five visits deep, and still not a positive result yet.

I know we're compatible with humans, as one of the other dragons I reached out to has a human partner of her own, and they've birthed two hatchlings together. DreamTogether assured me that genetically speaking, there should be no problem, though it might be a challenging pregnancy for the human.

I had to pay extra for that, but I don't mind. I haven't been hoarding for three hundred years for nothing. This is really a drop in the bucket—though I will have to fly home soon and get more things to pawn. I have a man now who's used to me, and has some connections with underground collectors.

I run my claws gently down her back, to the big swell of her ass and then to her pussy, which is gaping and leaking with me. She's lovely all full of me like this, used and still spasming. I lean down between her legs and extend my long, forked tongue to push my seed back into her, and she writhes.

"Again?" she asks, panting. Oh, it's tempting. But our session took so long—not that I'm complaining—that I think we're almost out of time.

"I would love to," I tell her, my tail winding up the bench to caress her thigh. "They may get grumpy with us, though."

She scoffs. "What are they going to do, drag you out of here?"

I chuckle and squeeze her again. "Hungry woman," I say, enjoying how she responds to my every touch. "Perhaps I should—"

There comes a loud knock. "Time is up," a voice says, and I sigh deep in my throat.

"I'm sorry," I tell her in a more sincere tone. Most of the time I'm trying to rile her up so her lovely cunt tightens up around me, but now I want to be honest with my feelings. "If I could, I would."

She just nods, and then I get a peek at her cheek as she turns her head. I love all of her big, voluminous black curls, how wild and free they are. They bounce with her slightest movement.

"I'm torn," she says, a little melancholy in her voice. "I'm sorry you have to keep paying and trying. But I always hope that there will be a next time."

I smile, even though she can't see it. "I know precisely

what you mean." My cocks slowly retract, until my slit closes up around them once more. "I have... enjoyed my time with you."

She swallows tightly. "Me, too."

"I'm sorry about this," I say, tapping the bench and making it rock. "Did I frighten you?"

Her hearty laughter fills the quiet, sterile room. "No. It scared me the first time, but not anymore."

That's a relief to hear.

I feel uncharacteristically bold, so I drop down onto my forelegs to lick her once more, from her clit to her ass, and she shakes.

"Don't wind me up," she says, a playful note in her voice.

"All right." I rise up again. "Thank you." I wish I had her name, but that's not why we're here. If she wanted me to know it, she would have figured out how to tell me already, despite the cameras listening and watching.

"Bye." She wiggles her butt, and I tap it once with my claw before stepping out of the room.

I do keep a home in the city, just so I don't need to fly far up north to my mountain every time I visit. The house is stark, with little furniture but built large enough to accommodate my size. I'm not sure who owned it before I did, but I have a feeling a bigfoot lived here, because I find long, brown hairs sometimes underneath the furniture that was left behind.

Between my sessions at DreamTogether, I often head to the other side of town, where a sassy imp named Rodney lurks in his dark little pawn shop. I bring things from my hoard that I'm willing to part with, and he tells me what he thinks he can get for them. He negotiates ruthlessly, starting at insulting prices before he'll get anywhere near what it's worth.

It frustrates me endlessly to say goodbye to these priceless treasures, but that's the cost of getting what I want.

The rest of the time, I simply wait. Dragons are good at waiting. We spend decades upon decades waiting. I eat when I need to, which normally isn't often—but after fucking my human today, and taking my time about it, I find myself absolutely ravenous.

I devour the bit of fresh meat left in the refrigerator, but it's not nearly enough, so I decide it's time to head back to my mountain tomorrow. It's time for another payment to DreamTogether, so I'll have to get another treasure for Rodney, which requires quite a lot of thought. Who knows how many more times I'll need to visit for my seed to stick? Before signing up, I went through the proper testing, and they determined I had a reasonable sperm count—though no other dragons have ever signed up, so they had little to compare to.

"Difficulty conceiving with monsters is fairly common," the clinician said at my last check-up. "Give it a few more tries, and then we'll investigate further."

Not that I'm complaining. Before this, I had only copulated a few times with others, notably a centaur woman I met in Italy when I was on a world tour. But it ended up being casual, and besides, I couldn't reproduce with her.

Perhaps it's vain, but I don't want to be the last of my kind. Our gene pool may be small, but there is still hope for us. I want to see dragonkind flourish again, to discover where we fit in the modern world. It does come with some amazing conveniences, after all, such as tiny computers that have access to all the information available on the planet, pretty much anywhere I choose to go. We even get reception at my mountain, though it's weak.

On my way home, I search the treetops for game trails, until I've located a herd of deer heading north. I swoop down, following them until they reach a small meadow before I fly in for the kill.

Once I've had my fill, I continue on into the flaming sunset until I see a familiar distant peak come into view.

My home. I've lived in this mountain for my entire life after inheriting it from my parents. My mother died, nearly two hundred years ago now, of the same disease that killed many of the other dragons of their age. My father, bound to her by the heart as he was, passed away soon after, as dragons usually do. Then I was left with the mountain in my care.

I've done my best to watch over it and the hoard they left for me since then. Some of it came from their parents centuries before, and there are many relics among the collection that I would never sell off to a pawn shop. Over time, I've arranged many of our greatest treasures into a sort of museum where I can appreciate these pieces of history. The sword of Genghis Khan. The armor of a long-dead samurai. A piece of Medusa's stone hair.

It is still hard to choose which piece will go next, which of these lesser treasures that serve as memories of my family will be the next sacrifice.

When I land on the ledge, the moon is shining and the stars are bright. As I step into the grand tunnel that leads deeper in the mountain, I think how marvelous this trip was, how much I enjoyed watching my cock slide in and out of my woman's beautiful body. How soft and yet powerful she felt around me, how each of her pretty moans and sweet cries drove me wilder and wilder.

I try to hold it back, so I don't hurt her, but sometimes I can't help myself with the way she milks me like her soft cunt is trying to suck me dry. I will never forget that, as long as I live.

Already my cocks are extruding just thinking about it, and I have to stifle a groan. Great. I'm not going to be able to sleep tonight unless I deal with this.

I wrap one hand around each of my cocks, and stroke them in alternating time thinking of her, those soft ass cheeks spread open for me, the lips of her marvelous sex stretched wide around me. I wonder what she looks like. Do her human breasts bounce the way her butt does? If I didn't have that big bench underneath her, would I hurt her in my rutting?

I suppose these questions don't matter, as I'll never have answers for them. I'll never know what she looks like, and I will never get to fuck her without the bench. I bet she's adorable, though, as most humans are with their squashed little faces.

Imagining what she might look like, I stroke all the way from the head of each of my cocks, down the shaft to the swell, and then wrap my claws around the base. That's where she held me tight inside her.

It doesn't take long for me to reach my finish, and I'm shocked by how much wet, white seed spurts out of me, decorating the floor of the cave.

Hell. Now I have to clean up.

three

SAMMY

DOING THE LONG DRIVE FROM DREAMTOGETHER BACK TO MY house in the boonies is my least favorite part of the trip. All I can think about is how wonderful my session was today, and how I wish I could do it more than once a month.

Soon the lights of the city fade, and I turn onto my little dirt driveway. I bought this place while I still worked my last job, wanting something as far away from other people as I could get. Don't get me wrong—I love people, especially my friends—but I prefer it on my own terms. Out here it's completely silent, and the stars are like thousands of tiny crystals glowing in the night sky.

My little aging house needs some work, and I've been doing what I can to keep up with its needs, but there's always something else to do. I park my dingy car halfway onto the yard, since there isn't a driveway, and step out into the hot summer sun.

I wonder what my dragon would think of my place.

Of course, I do a pee test every few days to see if it's stuck yet. I have a whole box of them from DreamTogether, even though the techs were quick to warn me that the tests aren't perfectly reliable, and every positive result needs to be verified in the clinic.

Still, they only show a single pink line. Negative. Part of me is relieved each time, because it means I'll get to go back and see him again.

Every week, I go in to DreamTogether for my check-up, where they take my blood and run some scans. Everything is as it should be, with even a nod of approval from the doctor when I explain my diet and exercise routines.

But I'm still not pregnant yet, as hard as we've tried.

I thought this would be easier. It's not that getting absolutely railed by an attentive lover with an extremely huge cock—two of them—is a big ask, but I worry that he's wasting money on something that might never work. I don't know him well, but from what I have seen, he's a good person. *Dragon?* He likes to be a little filthy when we fuck, but it's all just a character. Underneath he's sensitive and caring, and worries frequently for my comfort and pleasure.

Besides, it's nice to be getting a decent stipend to do, well... nothing, really. And damn, it's good to do nothing for a while.

I've been hustling since I was sixteen, when I worked as a delivery driver and courier. My folks didn't have much, and it was up to me to make a little extra and save up for my adult life. I went to a cheap state college, got a degree in International Politics, and then discovered it was worthless to me. I was never going to do the Civil Service exam, or work as a diplomat abroad. I knew it, my parents knew it, everyone knew it. My heart wasn't there.

At least in school I learned how much I enjoyed going to

the gym to work out my frustration and stress, and that paved a new path for me as a personal trainer.

I studied and studied, worked and worked, and built a business from nothing with my bare hands. I had dozens of clients, and I attended to them and their needs from sun-up to sunset. I was making a good living.

Until, five years in, the day came that I just couldn't anymore.

The constant need to smile and nod and hype them up, even when they treated me like furniture, even when they were sexist or racist or simply intolerable...

Eventually, it crushed me.

When I burned out, I burned out hard and fast, like a fucking comet headed down from space. I threw a fit at the gym, then told all my clients I was leaving in a single angry email. I might have even broken some things on the way out. I eviscerated my business, intent on finding something else to do with my life.

I just wanted to *rest* for a while.

It was like providence that a few weeks later, when I was wondering how I'd pick up the pieces and continue paying my mortgage, I found the advertisement for DreamTogether.

I know that I'm a fine physical specimen, and I take good care of myself. I eat my greens and watch my sugars. I run a few miles every other day, and drink plenty of water. I have good genes, good teeth, good eyes, and I'm taller than most women, too. Based on my size and health, the clinicians at DreamTogether decided that I would be the perfect match for the dragon.

Now I wonder if maybe they were wrong. It shouldn't take this long, should it? What if they made a mistake and there's something wrong with me?

Well, mistake or not, I'm going to keep attending the

sessions as long as the dragon wants to keep paying for them —or until he gives up on me and chooses someone else.

I detest that idea, and immediately banish it.

It's become routine now that when I get home from meeting with him, I sit down at the computer and look up pictures of dragons online to try and help me picture him. There aren't many photographs, because their number are so few, and most of what comes up are illustrations from books. From what I can find, dragons come in many colors, from gold to green to black. None of these must be my dragon, though, because I know what his hands and tail look like, and they're crimson red.

Briefly, I wonder if it would take me long to find him online—but that's violating the agreement I signed with DreamTogether. He wanted this anonymous, and that's why he signed up when he could probably have met someone on a dating app.

I mean, he's a dragon. That's fucking cool.

No, all he needs is someone to carry his hatchling, and help him bring forward another generation so that his species might live on. And he doesn't need to know who I am for that.

It's also routine that as the days pass after our session, I find I want him again, my dragon. I've started thinking of him as *mine* now, even though I know he's not. I have no idea what his life is like outside of that sterile room.

But I have a feeling he doesn't have a partner, the way he fucks me. I don't think he would be quite so attentive, even loving, if he was in a committed relationship with someone else. It would be much more mechanical.

I wish I could see him more than once a month. It's been nearly half a year now of this, and though we don't generally hold an extended conversation before we get down to business, I still feel like I... know him. He's gentle, but also gives in easily to his instincts. He cares for me in the way that he always ensures I'm ready for him, that I want what he has to offer, that he isn't hurting me. Even when he's consumed by need, he tries his best not to damage me.

Except for the bench today. Management wasn't pleased when they came in and found he'd ripped it right out of the concrete again.

"We might have to put together a special setup for the dragon," I overheard someone say as I was unstrapped and helped down from the bench. "So it can stand up to him."

Something about that strength is... incredibly hot. A beast with that much size and power, who can still be gentle and sweet and care for his partner's pleasure? I'm a sucker.

But as one week drags by since our last visit, and then two, a stone settles in my stomach. Still a negative result. How long can we keep doing this? When is he going to decide it's no longer worth it?

At least in the meantime, I'm good at keeping myself occupied. My house is falling apart, and it's needed repairs for some time—ones that I definitely couldn't pay for on top of student loans. In the meantime, though, I've learned some handyman skills from watching videos online, and I've started making much-needed updates to my house, replacing rotting wood and saving up for some new windows.

Now, I have much more time for my friends, who always complained before that I never went out with them. These days we see each other every weekend, going dancing, or hiking, or simply lounging in the backyard when the weather's nice. My friends Jared and Sarah, who have been together since we were all in college, are fascinated by my stories about the dragon—but now there's a complication.

I wonder if they'll assign me to a different monster when he finally gives up.

"They said it's not uncommon for it to take a while, right?" Sarah asks. "He won't pull out yet." Then all of us cackle.

I hope she's right, and he keeps believing this is worth it.

ZAKARION

I spend far too much time sorting through the hoard, trying to decide which priceless treasure I value the least. After much agonized deliberation, I finally choose one: a gold necklace studded with rubies that was acquired sometime during the Renaissance.

Then I head back to the city, toward the seedier part of town where I can find Rodney's shop. Here everything is tucked very close together, and I need to be careful with my broad wings as I descend to the street. When I land with a *thump*, I terrify a pair of goblins who look like they're on a date.

I have to stoop to get in through Rodney's door, where he sits behind his glass counter, sharpening his nails. He jumps up when he sees me, eagerness glittering in his little beady eyes.

"My favorite customer," he croons, his tiny, red body slithering up over the counter to stand on top of it. His long, spaded tail swishes back and forth in wide arcs. "What do you have today?"

Reluctantly I bring out the necklace. I don't hand it over

right away, though, dangling it in front of him just out of his reach. Rodney frowns as his little hands grab at it.

"Fifty thousand," I say by way of greeting.

The imp physically flinches, and rocks back on his heels. "Greedy today, dragon?" he asks, twirling his tail around one finger. "There's no way I'll pay that for this."

"These are whole rubies. Huge ones. Even if you scrapped the necklace, each of those jewels is worth ten."

He just shakes his head. "Twenty or nothing. This is going to be a bitch to find a buyer for, and I'll be running a real risk."

We argue like that, same as we always do, until he settles on thirty-five. Then he swipes the necklace out of my hands and bites down on the jewel to test it before dishing out my money.

This should be enough to last me a little while, at least.

Stashing my cash in my backpack, I head back to my house in town. This is where I'll wait for the phone call from DreamTogether—either telling me that we've succeeded, and my surrogate is pregnant... or that I'll have to go back again.

Though every appointment forces a harder and harder choice about which of my valuables to part with, I'm thrilled at the prospect of seeing my woman again. I don't know how long this can possibly last, but DreamTogether seems happy to take my cash—and I'm happy to keep coming in and trying.

Either we conceive a hatchling eventually, or I get to fuck my wonderful woman forever.

four

SAMMY

When my phone rings and the caller ID tells me it's from DreamTogether, all my muscles clench up. I answer it, hoping it's not what I fear.

"This call is to confirm your appointment for next Thursday," the robo-call says, and relief cascades through me. He wants to see me again.

The morning of my appointment, I spend a good two hours taking a shower and then putting product in my hair to get the very best shining, bouncing curls that I can. I even put on makeup, though the dragon can't see my face. I use lotion all over, so my legs and butt are as smooth as possible. I know how much he likes to squeeze me everywhere, as if he enjoys the sight of my rather plentiful butt bulging between his claws.

He appreciates how I look, when most of the time human men find me intimidating. I'm tall, Black, smart, and once upon a time, a business owner. They can't handle me—but the dragon can.

Honestly, with how thoroughly he fucks me once a month, I've found myself with very little interest in my own kind anyway.

Then it's time. I park outside the DreamTogether office, practically vibrating with my excitement. I sit in the waiting room until my name is called, studying who else is here. There's a pretty younger woman with long, braided black hair, and we chat a little about what brought us each to DreamTogether. She had a shitty job working fast food, and wanted something better for herself. This is her first appointment, and she's nervous and excited. I try to impart a few words of wisdom, then a clinician grabs my folder to lead me back to one of the breeding rooms.

Oh. This is different. Inside the tiled room, the usual bench has been replaced with a completely different device. This time, all I see is a massive steel table, with leather straps on the top, and a cushion right about where my ass would be if I were strapped down to it.

"I'm sorry," the clinician says as she leads me inside. "We had to come up with a completely different design for the dragon. This will..." She trails off. "You'll have to look at him."

I stare at her. "What? But isn't this all supposed to be, um, anonymous?"

She nods rapidly. "And it still will be! He won't know your name or anything about you, besides how you look."

I gape at the table, which is mounted on a steel column nearly a foot in diameter. It's bolted into another steel plate on the floor.

He definitely won't be able to destroy this.

I'm going to have to look at him. It's a good thing I put on makeup today.

I lie down on the table, and they strap me in. For a

moment, I feel like a bizarre science experiment. The cushion raises my hips up to make it easier for him to penetrate me.

I only have to wait for a minute or two before the door opens. A huge, red creature steps inside, and his yellow eyes, with long, slender pupils, widen when they see me.

"Oh." We stare at each other, and I take in the full sight of him. He *is* huge, probably nine or ten feet tall not including his massive tail. His neck is long, and he has a hefty snout with flared nostrils, and spiked ridges for eyebrows. He's bright red all over, but his throat and belly are a cream color. Softer ridges run down his back to the tip of his tail, which is now twitching behind him. He has huge wings that, folded up against his back, run from the top of his head down to the ground.

He's standing upright on his hind legs, and he's completely naked, but... there are no sexual organs visible on him at all. I know he has them, so where are they?

His eyes are taking me in, too, and his mouth hangs slightly open, revealing all of his sharp, white fangs. Wow. They're *long*, and remind me somewhat of a velociraptor. He could tear me apart with those.

And yet, I'm not afraid at all. It's him. It's really him, and I can see his face, and look into his eyes.

Oh boy. This is going to be intense—I just know it.

He approaches me slowly, like I'm a prey animal he might startle if he moves too fast. A long, black tongue with a forked tip darts out of his mouth and licks along his teeth, then vanishes again.

"This is new," he says cautiously, stopping a good six feet away. He studies me from head to foot again, and his lips tilt down. Is he unhappy with what he sees?

"Y-yeah," I say, as heat rushes up into my face in embarrassment. Is he still going to want to do the deed now that he knows what I look like? "I think they made this custom for you."

His lips tilt down further, and now I'm sure that I've disappointed him. My vision gets a little cloudy. The connection we had must be ruined for him since the seal of anonymity has been broken between us.

"They did this because of me?" he asks, voice a little choked. He shakes his head, like he couldn't be more disappointed. I can't stop the tear that slips free at the look on his face.

"I'm sorry," I say, because I can't think of anything else. "I know this isn't what you wanted, but—"

His eyes widen, and he steps closer to me, his frown getting even deeper. "Are you crying?" he asks, and his shorter forearms reach out towards me, and then stop mid-air. "Why are you crying?"

"Well, the whole point was that you didn't have to look at me, and now you do, and—" I choke for a second on my words. "I understand if you want someone else now."

Horror creeps across his long face. He rushes towards me and I cringe. My eyes squeeze closed, preparing for anything.

What I don't expect is the single cool claw on my cheek. I crack one eye, and find the dragon gazing down at me with immense sadness on his face.

"I am..." He bites his lip with his sharp teeth. "I am incredibly grateful to finally look upon you."

With tears still streaking down my face, I blink at him. "But you look like I kicked your dog," I say in a shaky voice.

"I am simply shocked that they would have to do this," he says, gesturing at the whole table. "It must have cost a lot of money to install."

So that's what he's worried about? That DreamTogether had to build in some extra precautions for him? My relief must show on my face, because my dragon gently returns my smile, like he's afraid of frightening me with the whole thing.

"I'm sure you're paying them enough that it's not a big deal," I say, trying to sound bright and cheery again. "I mean, I don't know how much this is all costing you, but it must be a lot. I think they can afford it."

Strangely, my dragon says nothing in response as he slides his claw down my cheek. It continues over my jaw, and along the exposed flesh of my throat. His breath hitches, and his eyes follow the path of his hand down my body as he reaches the curve of my breast. He doesn't touch it, though— he simply stares, like he can't believe what he sees.

"You're beautiful." His voice comes out a shallow whisper. "More beautiful than I could have imagined."

Wow. I didn't expect that. Now my face is getting hot for a completely different reason.

"May I touch you?" he asks abruptly, and I stare into his reptilian, yellow eyes.

"Oh. Um, sure."

His lips peel back on his snout in a grin. His claw traces the curve of my breast, to my sternum, and then back again to my nipple. He circles it gently, before placing his whole hand around it.

I try to hold in a tiny moan at just this faint touch, because it feels utterly electric. The dragon's eyes go even wider at this reaction.

That's when I see it: down between his hind legs, along the cream-colored scales of his belly, something is... opening. It's a long slit, and I can make out what looks like two objects hiding inside. I'm watching with unabashed interest as the two soft heads peek out, then grow, extruding farther and farther out from that slit.

"Oh," I say in surprise. "That's how those work."

The dragon glances down, then tries to cover it with one of his big hands. "Yes," he says shyly. "Not quite like a human."

I shake my head, wishing that I could move my arms, that I could take his hand away in mine and really get a good look at him.

"They're... nice," I say finally, not sure how else to put it into words. "Can I see?"

The dragon's mouth falls open, but then he snaps it shut and glances down as he pulls his clawed hand away. Two immense cocks now protrude from that pocket in his abdomen, and the shape of them—suddenly I understand why he feels the way he does inside me. His penises are certainly unusual, covered in small nubs, as I suspected. There's no foreskin, just soft scales covering the surface, from the softly-pointed head to the thick swell, down to the slimmer section where his two cocks jut out from his body. One is directed more upward, the other downward, and below them, I can make out two lumps under his flesh that must be testicles.

"Wow," I say, without realizing I'm even speaking. "So that's what they look like."

He tilts his head away and scratches his nose with his other claw. "Yes," he says uncertainly. "I understand if it's too strange for you."

I squint at him. "Of course it's strange. You're a dragon."

His lip quirks upward at the edge. "I am. And you are a human. A lovely human." This time, he touches both of my breasts at the same time, and he peers down at them with lowered eyelids. "These are how you'll feed my hatchling, aren't they?"

I hadn't thought much about that. If dragon babies drink milk, that is.

"I don't know," I say. That's when I'm supposed to give the *hatchling* back to him. But I don't want to ruin his little fantasy.

His smile widens as his claw circles my breast and then gently, sweeps over my nipple. I gasp. "Lovely. You'll feed it well."

Why is that so fucking hot?

Once he's explored my breasts, his hands drift downward, over my belly to the curls between my legs. My thighs are already spread wide for him, but he doesn't dip down right away. Instead, he tangles one of his claws in my hair.

"Human hair is so... cute," he says quietly, studying me there.

Never thought I'd hear that one. But the longer he observes me, the hornier I'm getting. Slowly his hand continues downward, the scaled pad of his finger glancing over my clit. I tremble, and now he's smiling so wide I can see all of his fangs. "You're wet," he observes, leaning closer to me so I can feel his hot breath spilling out his nostrils and onto my face. "Perfect for my cock."

There he is. My dragon is back, now that we're past the shock of the table, of seeing each other. When I glance down, I find dribbles of white pre-come sliding down both of his dicks, and I get even wetter.

His gaze follows mine downward, and then when we lock eyes again, there's an expression on his face that, even though he's a dragon, is very clearly a smirk. He reaches down with one of his big, clawed hands and wraps it around his upper cock. Then he strokes it, once, his fingers rolling over the nubs as he travels up and down.

Oh, how I can't wait to have those inside me again. I feel like I must have just vibrated from head to toe, and somehow he felt it through the floor, because he takes a step towards me so his chest is right up against my face.

"It's adjustable," I say, nodding to the left, where they said the control was. Curious, he reaches over and pulls the lever, which tilts my table back.

"Whoa." I wish for just a second I could move properly. But almost immediately, I realize why they do this for us.

The dragon puts two big, clawed hands on the table to either side of my face, then climbs up, his tail thrashing to keep balance and his wings flicking partially-open behind him. He blots out the fluorescent lights overhead as he clambers into the right position, his body on top of mine, his cocks now rather close to where the cushion is lifting my ass toward him. When I look up, he's peering down his ridged snout at me, a hint of concern in his eyes.

"Is this all right?" he asks, flattening his wings once again as he gets settled.

I nod quickly. "Yes, it's fine." Fuck. I probably should be terrified right now, but I'm horny out of my mind. I want one of those cocks again, just like I've been fantasizing about since last month. "Are you, um, ready?"

His eyebrows lower, and his grin reveals all of his sharp teeth.

"Oh, I'm ready to put a hatchling inside you," he growls, in a voice deeper than I've ever heard him use. His tail is twitching even more insistently behind him now, like an excited cat's. "Right now."

five

ZAKARION

I NEVER COULD HAVE IMAGINED JUST HOW PRETTY AND SWEET my little human truly is, not until now that I'm looking down into her face. She has big, dark eyes with long lashes, deep brown skin, and perfectly full lips. Her mouth is open and slightly round in surprise, revealing all of her shiny white teeth.

I'm already leaking for her. I want to continue observing her, trying out all the different parts of her, but I'm too eager, and my cocks want too badly to be inside her again. Yes, all they want is to slide into her warm, wet sheath and pump her full of me again.

I will attempt many times today to put my hatchling in her. They can knock on the door all they want.

"Hatchling," she repeats, and then those impossibly long lashes sweep lower over her eyes. "Please, put one in me."

Her body arches up toward my weeping cocks and instinctually I lower my hips, my legs adjusting where I have my claws wrapped around the rubber edge of the table so I'm much closer to that open space between her legs, the one that's calling for me. I can't wait to be inside her again.

I should have spent some time preparing her, but I was too excited once I laid eyes on her. Now my lower cock is nudging between the swollen lips of her cunt, spreading them apart and slathering my seed all over her. With a measure of control, I use my left hand to drag the knobby crown upward, over that little bead under her hood that I know brings her great joy. I make sure to apply my nubs as I drag myself up and down over it, and my woman lets out a hoarse moan.

"Oh, that's good," she whimpers, her hands flexing in their bonds. "But..."

"But...?" I prompt, repeating the motion and earning another gasp.

"Fuck me, please." She pushes her hips forward as much as she can, and my lower cock slips into her slit.

I let out a surprised groan as that cock, much less used to this sort of stimulation, croons its pleasure. Now my upper cock is positioned across her clit, trapped between us.

"Yes!" Just the textured head inside her has her calling out for me already, so I flex my hips, seating myself a measure deeper. "Don't play with me today," she says in a surprisingly helpless voice. Those dark brown eyes of hers are so bright as she gazes up at me that I'm utterly entranced. "I'm way too horny."

I nod quickly. Now that she's seen me, she's even more aroused? My ego is instantly aflame, and the scales on my back ruffle with pride. Even smoke pours out of my nose as I reposition my legs again so I can put more power behind my hips.

I know what she's after. Usually I'm slow to enter her, to

let her adjust her to me, but that's not what she wants today. I will give her what she craves.

With a forceful jerk of my thighs, I drive my cock deep.

"Ah!" She cries out so loud I worry that I've hurt her. She's so unbelievably wet, and squeezing so hard around me, that it's difficult not to thrust again, but I wait to make sure she's all right.

My woman frowns at me. "That's all?" she asks, her mouth curving up at the side. I return her mischievous grin and reel my hips back, then push into her a second time, just up to the halfway point. She's not ready for my swell yet, but she will be soon.

As I thrust, my upper cock drags over her clit, and she throws her head back. Her moan is deep and throaty, full of her pleasure. Her bow-shaped lips open in a perfect circle as I repeat the motion, this time reaching between us to push my cock down and apply even more friction to her clit.

The sound that bursts out of her surprises even me. Her eyes roll back in her head and her arms spasm in their straps as I thrust in again, giving her the same amount of pressure as before. Her entire body trembles under me, and most perfectly, her pussy clenches tight.

"I think that might just kill me," she gasps, looking up at me with half-lidded eyes.

"Does that mean you'd like me to do it again?" I ask, moving only slightly inside her with my breaths.

"Yes, you big dragon!"

Against my better judgment, I slam my cock into her, and her whole body shakes. She's even more open for me today than usual, and I slip in almost up to my swell.

I have to stop there and pause to breathe, because I'm already so close to finishing, and I want to see what she looks like when she meets me at the end.

Bracing myself with one arm and my legs, my free hand wrapped around the base of my upper cock, I pull out and then plunge back in, earning a moan or a cry with every stroke. As I had hoped, her big breasts bounce with every one of my movements, her broad, dark nipples pointed and erect for me. I curl my long neck down until my head is chest-level with her, and her eyes grow wide as I wrap my tongue around one of those perfect nipples.

She *squeals*. Her whole body arches, straining against her straps as I rut into her again and again, filling up her tiny body and shoving down my second cock to stimulate her even more.

"Are you ready?" I growl to her, bringing my lips up to her cheek, and then her ear. "I'm going to fit all of it inside you, and then I'm *really* going to fuck you."

A half-drunk smile crosses her face. "You know I am."

So I pump harder, squeezing even more of myself into her, and her mouth falls slack. Her body welcomes me, parting for me and then fluttering and trembling around me. I'm so lost to my pleasure that I let go of my upper cock, because I need both hands and both legs to fuck her.

Then she swallows me, up to the narrow point near my slit. I groan as I'm finally fully seated in her, and I'm in awe that she can take all of me. When I peer up into her face, her eyes are closed in bliss.

That's when I really test the new table for what it can take.

I snap my hips back hard, and then delve into her again, and again, and her cries become screams of pleasure. My balls are aching, and both my cocks are shivering with their need to release, but she's not there yet. I watch her face carefully as I fuck her even harder, yanking out my cock until it almost slips free, and then pushing it through her soft, swollen cunt, changing my angle as her cries rise and fall. Soon, she's tightening up blissfully around me, and I can barely hold on for a moment longer, when—

It hits her. Her whole body goes stiff as a rock, and her tiny channel clamps down tight around me. I let out a ragged moan as I fuck her through it, but I can't keep it in.

My orgasm erupts out of me like a volcano. "Oh, hell," I groan, slamming into her, and she ripples again around me, as if she just climaxed again. More of my seed shoots out, one vicious jet after another from both heads, and I'm still pumping inside her, trying to get as much of it deep into her as I can. I even feel flame billowing up in my chest, but I know better than to let that out in here.

Someday soon, my hatchling will grow inside her, and those incredible, wide hips of hers will wrap around it, cradling it until...

"That..." She takes a deep breath. "That was incredible. Holy shit."

I elongate my neck and then smile down at her, pleased that I can see her face after fucking her senseless. She's even more beautiful with her hair wild behind her, her cheeks darkened at the apples with exertion. Puddles of my seed cover her chest and belly, and she looks so good covered in it.

I lower my head and nuzzle her with my snout, and she giggles as some of her hair gets tangled in my fangs.

"Thank you," I tell her, as I gently withdraw my lower cock from her. We're both dripping, and I clamber off the table, then adjust the lever back to a position that might make her more comfortable.

Sometimes I wish we could do this without it. Would I hurt her if we tried?

"I hope it works this time," she says as my cocks both

slowly start to withdraw into my slit. She gives me a bit of a sad smile. "I bet this is costing you a lot."

I dislike the process of parting with my hoard, but it's worth it for this. "I am a dragon," I say with a shrug. "Don't worry yourself with it."

She tilts her head like she's not sure what that has to do with anything. I run one claw up her throat, to her chin, and tip her face so I can peer into her eyes.

"I am old," I clarify. "By your standards. I have plenty of wealth. What is the point of having collected it all if not to spend it where it matters most to me?"

She blinks, and then her smile falls a little. I'm not sure what I've said.

"Of course," she says. "Dragons hoard, right?"

I nod, and then a more forced smile returns to her face. "Thank you for today," she says. "I always enjoy this with you, even though that's not the purpose."

I furrow my brow at her words, not certain what they mean. But then the knock comes at the door, telling me my time is over.

"Bye," she says, with a little wave of her hand, and I leave the room wondering what happened.

SAMMY

For just a split second, I thought that what he meant by 'what matters most' was *me*.

But then I realized, of course it's not about me. This is about his species and his child. That's the only reason he's pouring as much of his *hoard* into this as he is.

He looked confused as he left, but after today, my heart feels a little wounded. Now that I've seen him, looked into his eyes as he slid that amazing cock of his inside me, I don't think I'll ever be the same again.

That night, instead of looking at pictures online and pleasuring myself, I curl up on the couch and watch an old movie, trying not to get emotional.

Of course I don't mean anything more to him. He's my client. I'm offering a service, that's all. It's what we both signed up for.

I thought this would be easier, given my history. Besides —it's just sex. I've played the "just sex" game before. So why would this be any different?

The next month drags on as I do more and more pee tests, slowly making my way through the box they gave me. And still, negative.

Negative.

Negative.

At my weekly check-ups, it's the same thing: not a fetus in sight.

It's a Friday night and I'm at home alone, drinking orange juice and pretending it's a screwdriver, when the rain starts. It pelts the house, one of those wild summer thunderstorms, rattling everything with the force of the downpour.

Then some of it starts to stream through my roof.

"Fuck!" I hop off the couch as water dribbles in rivulets from the ceiling, landing on my old carpet. I know I need to replace it, but this is not how I wanted to be forced into it.

Frantically I run outside, grab a bucket, dump it out and carry it back inside to put it under the drizzle—only for another spot to start leaking, too.

By the time the storm is over, I have a mixing bowl, a

bucket, and an empty crock pot all catching water and I'm frantically searching the internet for local roofers.

In the morning, I call someone to come take a look.

After he climbs back down the ladder and wipes his hands on his jeans, the roofer lets out a deep sigh. I know what's coming.

"Your roof's old," he says. "You'll have to replace the whole thing."

My heart stops cold as he starts drawing me up an estimate. I'm making decent money at DreamTogether, but not enough to cover an expense like this. Politely I pay for his time and wave goodbye as he drives off down the road, all those zeroes flashing in my head.

Just great.

That's when my phone rings. "This is to confirm your appointment for next Thursday..."

I sigh. At least there's that. It's not that I don't want to see my dragon again—it's that I'm afraid of how he makes me feel.

I don't know him at all, not really. I only know that one side of him, the side he shows me in that room, on that table. But now, being face-to-face... this has become dangerous very quickly. I like how filthy he is, and how caring and affectionate he is underneath it. I love his white fangs and reptilian eyes, his long tongue and clawed hands. I adore how his cocks emerge only when he's horny for me.

But I can't have him. Not only because of DreamTogether, but because of who we are. I'm human. I'll live seventy, maybe eighty years. If he's already been alive for a few centuries, how many more centuries does he have ahead of him? We're too different.

I could probably back out now. It's not too late, since I'm not pregnant yet. But I also want him to get his wish. I want him to have his hatchling, to have that future he clearly craves more than anything.

And I need the money, plus some, if I'm going to replace this stupid roof.

So I don't back out, and on Thursday, I walk into Dream-Together with a new intention not to let myself get attached to the dragon.

six

SAMMY

WHEN HE WALKS IN THE ROOM, I TRY TO LOOK AS BRIGHT AS I can, the way I used to when I had to go in to work at five in the morning to train an early bird client. It's my 'customer service' face, intended to put some distance between me and my client.

"Hi," I say, trying to flap one hand, though it's restrained to the table. "Nice to see you."

He pauses in the doorway, and tilts his head to one side. "You, too," he says, like he's confused by my greeting. He has hunger in his eyes as he takes stock of me, but then he pauses on my face. "Are you all right?"

"I'm fine!" I say, perhaps too cheerily. Those ridged brows of his lower as he closes the door behind him. He approaches me, surveying me from head to toe, and slowly his slit begins to part. His black tongue flicks out, licking over his teeth before vanishing back into his mouth.

This time, when he palms one of my breasts, I try not to look too closely at him, because looking at his face *does* things to me. When he slides his claws down between my legs, testing me out, I try to keep a straight face.

We're here for a reason, and the deeper this connection gets between us, the harder it will be to part.

When I don't give much of a reaction, the dragon rises back to his hind legs, and studies me with his head tilted.

"Well?" I ask, nodding toward the adjustment lever.

His frown deepens, but he does what I ask, tilting the table so he can better climb on top of me. This time, there's no begging. There's no dirty talk. That frown remains on his face as he takes his upper cock this time and fits the tip inside me.

Oh, does he feel good. But I try to keep it out, to wall myself off from how incredible he feels, how intimate this is, and keep my head turned.

Suddenly, he slows down. When I look at him, his expression is one of deep worry.

Then he pulls out.

"What is it?" I ask, growing concerned myself. "Am I not doing a good job?

He backs away from the table. "You're not here." He shakes his head, and looks away from me. "I can't do this if you're not here."

Fuck. Is he going to... *fire me?*

"I am," I say, with as much sincerity as I can muster. "I am here. Right here, and you're going to fill me up with a hatchling, right?"

The dragon studies me with those piercing yellow eyes and the long, black pupils. His nostrils flare, then, with a sigh, he nods. He clambers back onto the table, and this time, he doesn't look at me either as he fucks me.

He still feels so good, but the sizzle has evaporated between us. We go for a long time while he tries to make me orgasm, and eventually, I do, as unnecessary as it is. Then he releases inside me with a low grunt. Very little come trickles out of his upper cock where it lies over my belly.

Once he's regained his breath, the dragon pulls out and gets back off the table, using the lever to return it to its original position. His shoulders are slumped as his cocks retreat back into their place inside him. He didn't gush inside me, like he usually does. Only a few drops leak out when the table tips me forward again.

"Thank you," I tell him, smiling. He doesn't return it.

His lips are turned down and his brow is furrowed as he finally says, "Well, next time, then?"

I nod in agreement, and he waves at me weakly, then vanishes out the door.

ZAKARION

My human was someone else today, and I didn't like it. Not at all.

It was as if she had carved a wooden cut-out of herself and left it in her place. There was no magic, no affection, just professional politeness. Even when I teased her body the way she likes, she wouldn't look at me.

As I leave DreamTogether and spread my wings, I wonder what I've done wrong. I launch into the air and fly home, my heart sinking deep into my gut.

Has she changed her mind? Does she no longer want to do this?

Does she dislike me for something I don't remember doing?

That night, I curl up in the bedroom of my house, where I moved out the bed and built a nest from some blankets and pillows instead. There, I go over everything that happened today, and everything that happened last time, to try to deduce where I misstepped. But I don't know where I crossed an unmarked line. What made her put on that fake, shallow version of herself, when I know there's so much more underneath?

I feel dirty all over for how I took her today. It was a transaction, nothing more, and she made that clear enough.

That's when I realize that I'm an idiot. A fucking idiot.

I was the one who thought this meant more to her than just a job, but that's clearly not the case. She's being paid to be there, to be my vessel. That's all this is, and I was a fool to think it was anything else. She was just trying to tell me that.

It takes eons for me to fall asleep, and it's bright and early the next morning when I get a call.

"What is it?" I ask, yawning as I hold the tiny phone to my ear.

"Zakarion?" says a man on the other end, with a gruff, deep voice. "Is this the dragon, Zakarion?"

"Yes, that's me." I yawn again and climb out of my nest, stretching my neck and tail as far as I can. "What is it?"

"I'm with the Department of Antiquities. Are you the prior owner of the Goblet of Hilumeni?"

What? No one should know about that. Well, no one except Rodney, the pawn shop owner, and I. It was the goblet I sold to him a few months ago for enough cash to keep paying DreamTogether.

"Why?" I ask, guarded.

"Because this is an item of international interest," the man says in a tone that's almost... threatening. "And you sold it under the table to an imp for fourteen thousand dollars."

I mean, I know I was taking a bad price, but Rodney was the only one who would pay cash.

"So?" I ask. I don't know what business it is of anyone else's.

"That violates a number of international treaty laws. This is a protected item. It has been seized, and we would like to ask what other invaluable cultural artifacts you're planning to sell on the black market."

"Black market?" I growl into the phone. "What are you talking about? It's mine to do with as I want."

But I already know where this is headed.

"What else is there?" the man on the other end presses. "We can't prove yet that the goblet came from you, but if you try it again..."

Fuck. That was my plan for my future hatchling. Though I've already paid for the full package at DreamTogether, each of the breeding sessions costs extra.

But now? It's all over.

I hang up the phone, no longer listening to the man on the other end. I'm going to have to find a new pawn shop to sell my wares, or dig further underground, which doesn't sound appealing.

Hell, I don't know. I'm too old for this. And that means parting with even more of our ancient treasure, my links to my past and my family.

No. Perhaps... perhaps this is a sign. After my poor showing yesterday, and the coldness of that room, it might be time to throw in the towel. What I have with my human will never be anything else, nothing beyond our occasional meetings in the breeding room. It will never be the closeness and connection I'm imagining.

Will she give me that empty, fake-happy face again when I tell her?

The threatening man tries to call me again, but I silence it and stash the phone in my bag. I hope Rodney hasn't spilled what other treasures he's fenced for me, too, or I could be in real trouble.

I decide to retreat to my mountain earlier than usual. I need the fresh air, the sunshine, the cool comfort of my hoard—which is now mostly useless to me. And I need to be far away from the government's prying eyes until things cool down.

I suppose I could dig out some raw gold coins and sell those above-board, but there's no point any longer. It was never going to work for me at DreamTogether. I have one last appointment already paid for, and that will be the last.

After chasing down some prey in the woods and devouring it whole, I stretch out over the immense pile of treasure I've accumulated in my many years. My mind keeps flitting back to that moment in the white tile room, how my human kept her head turned away while I... what?

While I *what*? While I made love to her?

That's not what this is. I hired her for a reason. I went to DreamTogether because I don't need a partner—just a hatchling that I can devote my life to raising. There's no emotion involved in any of this, and she knows that.

I should know that, too. Maybe that's what she was trying to tell me with that pasted-on smile: that we went too far last time.

I'm not surprised when I never receive the call. If it hasn't worked yet, what makes me think that poor showing I put on at our last session will make a difference? Whenever I think of it, my cocks shrivel even further inside me.

Finally, I drag myself up to my feet and head out to the landing, then spread my wings. Time to return to civilization, and give notice to DreamTogether that it's over.

I won't get my money back on the package, unfortunately, but I find I don't care that much about the money. It's my human who I won't see again. It's the memory of her pert, round nose and soulful, brown eyes that drives a dagger through my belly.

SAMMY

I feel awful about it after seeing the dragon's face as he left, but it's the right thing to do. DreamTogether put boundaries in place for a reason, to protect our clients. I already let this go too far, probably the very first time the dragon came in and introduced himself to me with no name. I was too open with him, too receptive to the affection he lavished on me.

I wasn't a *professional* about it, and now that's back to bite me in the ass. It was always our mantra in the gym: kind, friendly, attentive, and professional, no matter what. Even when you have your hands on someone's ass while you try to balance them on a workout ball, you were professional, professional, *professional*.

It's been getting colder out lately, so I know I have no choice but to fix the roof before it starts to snow. I pay what I can so the roofers can get started, hoping the dragon doesn't cancel our next session.

But the guilt eats at me as the tests still come up negative. He has all of his hopes for the future of dragons pinned on this.

I wonder what's wrong? There isn't much online about dragon fertility—only that the population has been in decline for some time, and few new hatchlings have been born since the 70s. I look up everything else I can, including how lizards mate, to see if I can discover a solution, but all I learn is that they're highly sensitive animals.

The day of the appointment, I'm strapped onto the table that's held up well enough so far. It helps when he isn't desperately fucking me with everything both of us are worth. I wish I could bite my nails as I wait for him to come in, because all I can think about is his dejected face as he left last time.

Then the door opens. In steps one long, crimson leg, and behind it, the dragon appears in the doorway, all nine feet of long neck and claws and fangs. His tail looks stiff behind him as he walks in, and his brows tilt down as he studies me.

"Hello," I say brightly, but all this does is appear to upset him more. He closes the door behind him, then walks towards me until we're face to face at a polite six feet apart.

"I'm not going to mate with you today," he says, before he's even greeted me. The smile falls from my mouth in my surprise.

"What?" My body feels heavy. He really is going to fire me. "Why not?" A spark of panic flares to life. But I've gotten so used to this job, and I need the money right now. I can't—

"It is nothing against you," he says, his eyes sliding away from my face. I don't know him that well, but it sounds like a lie. "I've run out of money."

I can almost breathe again, but perhaps this is worse, because then I can't convince him to keep trying.

"I thought you had a hoard?" I ask tentatively.

He shakes his head. "It's now without any value," he says, his tone a little guarded. "I can no longer pay."

I search his yellow, reptilian eyes for some sign that this isn't true, that we're not done. Now I regret last time immensely. He won't even use his last appointment. We're out of time and out of chances.

"I'm sorry," I say, lowering my head. "I know this was a dream of yours. That there aren't many of you left. I know it was—" I'm surprised when my own voice comes out choked. "—important to you."

He looks resigned. "I don't know if it was going to work anyway." His tail curls around his feet, like he's protecting himself. "Perhaps it wasn't meant to be, at least, not for me. I was not intended to have a hatchling." He rubs the back of his head, his neck hanging low, making him look even smaller.

"Of course it's meant for you," I say, almost harshly. His eyebrows rise. "You're sweet, and kind, and gentle. No one deserves a baby more than you."

It's all true. Faced with the threat that we might not see each other again, I have to admit that he's become incredibly special to me, and so has his mission. He invested so much in this, the idea of having a child of his own, and now that dream is crushed.

Confusion settles on his face. "I thought I had offended you," the dragon says. "Is that not the case?"

I blink at him, equally perplexed by his question. "Offended me? No, of course not. You've been nothing but a gentleman. A... gentle-dragon." I offer one of my most enthusiastic customer service smiles, but when I do, he frowns deeper.

"I see." He lifts his chin and his expression hardens. Whatever's happened, my attempt to play happy and friendly is having the opposite effect on him. "I suppose our business is concluded, then."

What? No. I can't let him leave like this.

"Wait," I call out as he turns around. I wish I could pull out of these damn straps and reach towards him. I want him to stop and just think for a moment. "What are you going to do?"

He pauses, but doesn't look back at me. "Nothing. I will return to life the way it was before I met you."

He doesn't say *before DreamTogether*. No, it's before *me*.

It's infinitely sad to see him like this, hardened and hopeless. I don't like it. He's cheerful and considerate and open, optimistic about the future of his species.

I open my mouth to speak again, but I don't know what to say. That I don't want him to go? That I want a proper goodbye?

Instead of any of those things, I say, "Let me help you." It just comes out, but the moment I say it, it's all I want. I'm not ready to say goodbye to him, and I don't want him to give up.

Now the dragon does turn to me, one eyebrow lifted. "You have helped me enough," he says. "It was never going to work."

"But we were both tested!" I say, helplessness creeping into my voice. "There's no reason it shouldn't work. It just needs more time to—"

"There is no more time." The way he says it isn't harsh, but final.

"There's no more time *here*," I counter. "At DreamTo-gether. But..." I know what I'm about to say is crazy—crazy and probably stupid. "But there's plenty of time if we, um, left."

Those reptilian eyelids of his rapidly blink. "Left?" he echoes.

"Yeah. What if we..." I flounder for the right words. I know that DreamTogether is listening, but if he's going to terminate today anyway, then who cares? I'm certainly not going to be bred by a stranger, another monster, after this. I only want him, and it would feel strange, wrong, with anyone else. "What if we met outside of here?" I finally ask. "Maybe it has something to do with this room. We could try it somewhere else, and see if that makes a difference."

Am I really offering what I think I'm offering? To keep doing this, even outside the company?

Yes. Yes, I am. I think my dragon deserves everything he wants and more. And the truth is that I'm not ready to let him go.

"You want to continue this?" he asks, aghast. "I couldn't pay you. And what if they get upset with us?"

"So what? What are they going to do about it? Once your business is concluded with them, they're not the boss of either of us any longer."

He studies me, his neck elongating towards me as he tries to read my face.

"You would do that?" he asks, a hint of hopefulness in his voice. "Truly?"

I nod. "I would. You should have what you want."

"What does that get you?" he asks, his eyes narrowing as he turns back around to face me. "This is your job."

I wish I had an answer for that. I have no idea what I'll do, but I've always been a hustler. I'll figure it out.

"Leave that to me," I say at last. "I can handle it."

Still, the set of his mouth is uneasy. "It doesn't feel right to—"

"You're still arguing with me?" I pull on the strap holding me down. "Do you want my help or not?"

His tail thrashes behind him, like he's thinking hard and doesn't know what to say. His wings even extend a little, then readjust and return to their resting place.

At last, he says, "I do. I do want your help." He crosses the distance between us, and I inhale sharply as he stops right in front of me. He raises one clawed hand to my cheek and strokes it with one of the sharp tips. "More than anything."

"Then let me help," I say more firmly. "And get me the fuck out of this thing, will you?"

seven

ZAKARION

She's willing to help me, without compensation.

I wonder what I'm missing. Her emotions seem to sway back and forth like the sea. Last time we were in this room, it was as if she didn't know me. Now she's offering to... loan me use of her body, for nothing in return?

I don't understand, but her face is so vulnerable and pleading that I know I have only one choice.

Using my claws I free her arm from the strap, even though we could easily have called in someone on staff to help.

"What's your name?" she asks as I cut the strap on her other arm.

Oh, of course. Now that we're tossing aside DreamTogether, there's no reason to keep who we are secret anymore.

"Zakarion," I say. "Offspring of Zabaza and Akatarion." I draw her arms forward to hold onto my shoulder while I reach down to free her legs. When I've helped her down to the floor, I realize precisely how *small* she is. How does a creature this size take my cock? And take it so well?

"You are?" I ask as she plants both feet on the ground and straightens.

"Samantha," she says. "Sammy. I prefer that."

I taste the sound of her name. "Sammy." It's cute, like she is. Cute and precious. I resist the urge to touch her now that she's freed of the table. I want to pick her up and clutch her close to me, but she's keeping a safe distance, so I do, too.

"Shall we get the hell out of here?" she says, heading to what appears to be a locker in the back of the room. She opens it and grabs her clothing.

All I can do is nod, because I'm not sure what's happening. We're really... running off together. I watch as she slides on her underwear, bra, shirt and pants.

"So many clothes," I observe while she dresses.

Sammy purses her lips. "When you have tits like mine, you need 'em." She slams the locker closed, then approaches me. "Let's go, *Zakarion*."

Oh, I like that.

"Of course. Sammy." The taste of her name is delicious.

She grins, and leads the way. We don't even stop at the receptionist desk as we go. Sammy just flaps a hand over her shoulder, saying, "Sorry. I think we're done."

I'm pretty sure there will be some paperwork to sign later because I've violated the rules, but I'll let her have her moment. There's always paperwork. I'm rather amazed by her as I follow her from the building out into the autumn sunlight.

"Well," Sammy says, stopping abruptly. "Would you like to meet me at my house?" She tilts her head up to observe my full height. "I have a big backyard. We can figure out our plan of attack there."

I blink. *Plan of attack?*

"Lead the way," I say. "I'll follow your car."

She arches an eyebrow. "They let you do that?" she asks. "Just fly over town like that?"

"Who's going to stop me?" I shoot back, and she laughs.

I follow Sammy's hatchback out of the city, into the countryside. She pulls off the road onto a dirt trail, which leads to a cute, rather small house at the end. There's a shed, an abandoned swing, and a big yard of grass that got brown over the summer.

Seeing where she lives, I understand quite a bit more about Sammy now. She likes her freedom, and she doesn't want her neighbors seeing into her space. It's probably inexpensive to live here, and as I survey the house, it's clear she's recently repainted it, and the frames around the windows have all been replaced.

"This is lovely," I say, peering at the final flower blooms that are slowly starting to wilt in their beds. "All yours?"

She shrugs. "Some belongs to me, some to the bank still. If I'd kept my old job, I'd be a lot closer to owning it, but..." Sammy trails off. "Anyway, come sit down. I'll get us lemonade." She gestures at four yard chairs assembled around a table. When she goes inside to fetch the lemonade, I try to fit into one of the chairs, but it's far too small for me. Instead, I set it aside and sit on the ground, and I'm still tall enough that when Sammy returns and sits, I can look her in the eyes.

As she sips her lemonade, I cough. "How will helping me help you pay off your house?" I ask.

"It doesn't." She smiles, and it's a genuine one. "But that's okay. I'm not a stranger to rustling up some extra bucks here and there while we're working on our project."

"What would we be doing?" I ask.

Sammy furrows her brow like I'm daft. "Well," she says, coughing as she turns her head. "I mean, obviously. You'd be, you know." I've never seen someone look so embarrassed. "Trying to get me pregnant?"

"But if it didn't work at DreamTogether..." I begin.

"In that creepy white room?" she asks. "I read that lizards' bodies are sensitive to just about everything, from light to temperature. Some animals need perfect conditions to successfully breed."

Oh. I hadn't thought of that. But I know very little about my own kind, as my own parents passed away before I ever thought to ask.

"So perhaps it was too cold?" I say.

"Or your body didn't like the artificial lighting. Maybe you need sunshine."

I peer up at the sky, where the afternoon light is coming in through the leaves of the trees that surround Sammy's little house.

Is she suggesting...? My mind goes momentarily blank.

"Here?" I ask, like a fool.

"Why not?" Sammy rises from her chair, then pauses. "But we have to set some ground rules."

I don't like the sound of that. "DreamTogether was full of rules," I say, curling my shoulders.

"Right. It was to protect us." She rubs her arm. "And maybe we still need protection."

I give her a baffled look. "From what?" Does she think I'll injure her?

"From each other." She sighs. "It's easy to get too close when you're having sex with someone, you know? But that's not what either of us is looking for. What we want is to get you a hatchling, so dragons will continue after you."

I'm not entirely sure what distinction she's trying to make. "Are you speaking of romantic involvement?" I ask, just to be clear.

"That's what was brilliant about DreamTogether, right?" she says brightly, almost unnaturally so. "They connected us, but once our roles were played, that was the end of it. No complications."

So that's what she wants—for us to go our separate ways once the mission is achieved, without any further attachment. I try to ignore the way my heart plummets.

"Why do you smile that way from time to time?" I ask her, tilting my head. "It doesn't seem like you."

Her lip twitches, and the smile falls from her eyes. "What do you mean?"

"The way you looked at me as if..." I scratch my chin with one claw. "As if you didn't know me."

She shoots me a surprised look. "Oh." Her mouth tilts down into a frown. "It's... professionalism, you know? At my old job, we had to be professional, no matter what. And that's how I'm going to approach this, too."

So this is still just a part of the job for her.

But I believe I understand why she doesn't have romantic interest in me. Likely she would prefer to marry another human, spend her life with someone who would live a normal life at her side. I would live long beyond her, anyway.

We are not compatible. So, instead of letting that disappointment in, I nod and wall it off.

"I understand," I say.

"Friends?" Sammy asks, holding out her hand toward me.

I take it in mine, my big claws dwarfing her small palm, and we shake as best we can.

"Friends," I agree. And it tastes like ash on my tongue.

SAMMY

Way easier said than done, of course. Interacting with Zakarion out here, in the real world, he's even more... I don't know. Wonderful. Funny. A little out of his element.

Which, of course he is. He's a three-hundred-year-old dragon standing in my backyard. And now we've just shaken on our deal.

"Does that mean that I should, erm..." Zakarion's hand curls at his side, and the tip of his tail is twitching.

"Fuck me?" I ask. "Probably."

He looks up at the sun and spreads his wings, as if soaking all of it in. Then he approaches me, those wings still unfurled, and dwarfs me in their shadow.

"Are you certain?" His voice is lower, more full of gravel. "There is no steel table here to protect you."

Little does he know that's part of the fun.

"I have you here," I say. "You won't hurt me."

He doesn't look quite as certain as I feel, though. But he rises up on his back legs anyway, and he slips a claw under my shirt.

"Take this off," he says, in a way that's surprisingly commanding. This part of him is back, then. I peel up the shirt, not that it's necessary to the business of *procreating*, but I can't stand the way we did it last time. Mechanical. Businesslike. Zakarion needs intimacy to get turned on, and I don't mind the skin-on-skin with him, either.

I toss the shirt aside along with my bra, and then Zakarion nudges again with his claw at my pants. I can see that slit at his groin opening, revealing two hidden treasures inside. The moment I ditch my jeans, I stoop down in front of him.

"Sammy?" Zakarion asks, uncertain.

"Finally," I say, stretching my neck and my fingers. "I can touch you. I've always wanted to touch you."

His eyes get much bigger as his cocks begin to extrude, the twin heads pressed against one another until they're free of the pocket, and there, they spring apart—one pointing upward, the other downward, in that perfect way that stimulates me no matter which cock I take.

Two for the price of one.

I hover there, not quite touching him, and glance up. Here I was just talking about professionalism.

"Can I touch them?" I ask. I want to get him good and turned on before we do the deed—not to mention that I've always wanted to get up close and personal with his equipment, if it weren't for that damn table.

He gives me a sharp nod. "Please," he answers with a huff of hot air, smoke escaping his nostrils.

I close the distance between me and those two swollen, red cocks, and gently take the upper one in my hand. Now I can get a really good look at it, covered in the gentle nubs that feel like heaven when he fucks me, the smooth crown with the lip and no foreskin. I drag my hand downward, over the textured bumps, to the swell farther down.

"Oh hell," Zakarion grunts, pitching forward. He grips the edge of the lawn table like the tiny thing is holding him up. I stroke again, and beads of white form at the slit on each of his cocks. Sliding my hand from head to base, squeezing when I reach the swell like I imagine my pussy does around him, causes him to groan and his whole body to shiver underneath me.

But I can take it up a notch. If this is doing it for him...

I lean down and lick the white stuff right off.

"Sammy?" he asks, a hint of concern in his voice. Instead of answering, though, I lick again, and his hips snap forward, shoving his cock into my mouth. This time I take the whole head, then I raise my other hand to his lower cock so I'm double-fisting him.

"Fuck," Zakarion moans, the table creaking as he puts his weight on it. "That's incredible."

I swallow even more, then drag my lips back up to the tip again, sucking in while I do it. He's so responsive that I want to torture him even more, so I begin moving my hands in unison, dragging up and down along both his lengths while I take that massive cock into my mouth. I can barely reach the halfway point, though, before he's too wide to fit.

How on earth do I take this thing inside me?

"Sammy," Zakarion says abruptly, sounding choked. "Stand up."

Curious, I release him and do what he says, getting to my feet. Suddenly, his huge hands scoop me up, then seat me gently on the table, which is cold and hard under my ass. Zakarion hovers over me, his long neck bent to bring his snout near my face. He yanks my legs apart, exposing me to the backyard. His cocks are both pulsing, both hungry for me, both calling my name.

"I'm not going to waste it in your mouth," he says, panting. "I have to put it inside you."

I nod rapidly, and raise my hips up towards him, asking for what we both want. He guides his lower cock into me this time, the cone-shaped head easily slipping through my layers. His claws have found their way through the iron swirls on the table, and he grips them tight as he slides in deeper, reuniting with me again.

That's what this feels like, as Zakarion's eyes hover half-lidded, his big jaws open while his upper cock drags over my clit: coming back somewhere I belong. Drool pools at the base of his fangs as he pushes in, taking his time, like he always does.

This is what happens when you have sex with a creature that's hundreds of years old. He knows how to take his time.

"Zakarion," I manage to say as he begins to spread me wide, then retreats again. "Fuck me like you mean it."

At first, his yellow eyes get big, but then a smile curls his lip, revealing white, sharp teeth.

"Oh, I'll fuck you until you scream."

eight

ZAKARION

I'm mesmerized as my lower cock slips into her, and that tiny, dark brown slit of hers opens wide for me. I fist my upper cock in one hand to apply pressure as I slide it over her clit, and her hips reflexively buck under mine.

"Please," she begs, her heels hooking over my hips. "More. More."

I can't deny her anything, so I push even deeper, and miraculously her tiny body fits me inside it. I sag forward on the table, my testicles already aching, tingles of pleasure spidering out from where we're connected to every last one of my scales. Sammy lets out a cry, and I'm glad that her neighbors are a good distance away as I pull out of her, then slam back in again. Her tight sheath stimulates every last nub on my cock, and I groan as I shove myself farther into her, letting her swallow me.

This is the way it should be, I can feel it in my bones. Her wet heat pulsing around me, squeezing me, her big, brown breasts bouncing each time I yank my cock out and then thrust it back into her again.

Friends. Sammy made it clear to me what she wants, and I should want it, too. I will long outlive her, as will our hatchling. It makes no sense to bond, to have any more than friendship, or it will inevitably end in heartbreak for me.

"Zakarion," she gasps, clutching my arms tight in her fingers. Just the sound of her needy voice is driving me deeper, escalating the ripple of bliss running up and down my spine, all the way to the tip of my tail. I groan as she clenches me like a vise, and I don't know how my swell will possibly fit inside her—but the more I fuck her, frantically burying my cock in her delectable cunt, the more of it squeezes through. Her moans rise higher and higher, until she's crying out with every single pump of my hips.

"Open up for me," I murmur to her, curling my claws even tighter in the cheap little lawn table. "Let my cock inside you."

Sammy whimpers and spreads her legs wider, and I lean even closer to her, my hot breath blowing back some of her bouncy curls. This time, when I press into her, the swell of my lower cock slips through.

This time, she screams. I yank it out, then push in again, admiring her face as it contorts in pleasure. She reaches down between her legs and shoves my upper cock down, pressing it once more against her clit. The sensation of her cunt around one of my cocks and her hand on the other is almost too much for me to bear, and I groan as I pound into her over and over, trying to keep my own climax at bay.

But I don't need to hold out for long. Suddenly, Sammy's screams come to an abrupt halt, and her eyes fly wide, her mouth dropping open in a perfect circle. She clamps down around me so viciously that I can't help it any longer.

I roar as my own peak strikes me, hurling me into the void. I thrust into her once, twice, three more times, and then I explode. My lower cock squirts one burst of seed into her after another, while my upper cock splashes up her belly and chest. Under my claws, the lawn table has sagged, conforming to my powerful grip. Sammy moans raggedly, her cunt fluttering and twitching around me as I finally come to a stop, both of us panting hard.

I'm surprised when her hands sweep up my shoulders to my neck, and there she curls them around me, bringing me closer to her. She leans upward, so our noses are almost touching, and closes her eyes to rub her face against my snout.

It's so precious that I think I might melt into a puddle of dragon.

"Thank you," she murmurs, shivering with each of her heavy breaths.

I shake my head. "I should be thanking you," I say, reaching up with one claw to brush her hair back from her face. "You're the one doing this with me. *For* me."

She smiles and leans into it. "Well, someone has to make sure dragons don't go extinct. I want to be a part of that."

I sigh with post-coitus relaxation, and lean my forehead against hers. "You don't have to do that. You have... a whole life outside of this."

"I want to." She shrugs. "DreamTogether was my plan. But I don't want to get thrown at another monster. I want to see this thing through to the end with you."

I don't know what I did to deserve this woman's loyalty, but I won't squander it.

SAMMY

As promised, he did make me scream. I almost couldn't stand how delicious he felt inside me, how thoroughly I wanted—needed—to be taken by him.

Gently, Zakarion pulls out of me, and his thick come gushes everywhere. I stumble away from the table, which is now completely bent.

"Wow," I say, sweeping some of his fluid up in my fingers. "That was a lot." I remember our cold, emotionless session at DreamTogether, when he summoned just a few drops. He clearly needs affection and connection to perform best.

Zakarion grunts as he finally releases the table and stands up, towering over me with his long neck. The slender tip of his tail wraps around my leg, and I don't know if he does it consciously or not, but it's adorable.

"You bring it out of me," he says, glancing away as he scratches the ridges that run down his head and back.

I'm gratified that I can turn him on so much. It bodes well for our quest.

After going into the house to clean up and putting my clothes back on, I find Zakarion lying in the grass, soaking up the sun. He's huge, his long neck extended and his tail curled around his body. He looks like an iguana stretched out on a branch.

One of his eyes cracks open as I sit down beside his head, and his big reptilian pupil widens as it takes me in.

"Though I prefer you without clothing, what you've chosen is lovely," he says, languidly stretching.

I giggle. "Thanks. I don't usually dress cute, because most of the time I'm getting dirty."

"Dirty?" He quirks a brow. "Doing what?"

She gestures to her house. "Just keeping up with this old

thing. There's always some new crack to fix or rusty pipe to replace. You should see my collection of overalls."

His smile pinches his eyes. "I'm positive that you would look cute even in dirty overalls."

I can't help but grin. My dragon sure is a sweet-talker.

"How long have you lived here?" he asks, examining the ancient swing set. "Do you... have children?"

I laugh uproariously. "No, no. It was here when I moved in, and I saw no reason to get rid of it. Swinging helps me think sometimes, though I do worry often that it might collapse on me."

His mouth falls open. "Sounds dangerous."

I love how seriously he takes everything. His sincerity is so genuine and unassuming, it's a breath of fresh air. This is a dragon who has never put on a mask in his life.

"Do you want children?" Zakarion says after a long moment. I can't read the expression on his face.

"I don't know." I shrug. "It's never felt like an option for me, I guess? My life has never been stable, and when it comes to dating..." I trail off.

He blinks. "When it comes to dating... what?"

"I'm not good at it. Truthfully, I've always wanted to get married, ever since I was little." I sigh. "But I'm still looking for my perfect man."

His lips curl downward, but he nods in understanding.

"He's out there," Zakarion says. "And maybe then you will want to have children."

Maybe he's right. But it would have to be the right person, someone who made me want nothing more than to create life with them.

"Probably so," I answer. "Maybe subconsciously that's why I bought the house with the swing."

After a quiet moment, Zakarion says, "I suppose I should

return home." One of his hands curls behind my back, dragging a claw over my hip. Then, he freezes, and draws it away. "My apologies."

I blink for a moment, unsure why he's apologizing, until I realize just how affectionate of a gesture that was.

Offering him a smile, I say, "It's all right. We were just, um, pretty intimate."

He lifts his long neck up off the ground and nods curtly. "I will try to keep it at a minimum."

My heart falls a little at this, but I understand. It's what I asked for—and it's best if we keep an emotional distance between us, even when we're doing something so... personal.

Zakarion rises to his feet again, sitting up on his hind legs as he typically does. "Thank you," he says again, earnestly. "I don't know how I could repay you for this without—"

I wave a hand at him. "We already discussed this. You can't pay, but I want to help you anyway." Besides, the sex is incredible, and now I'm committed.

Zakarion searches my eyes, puzzling over me, before nodding. "If you're certain," he says, sounding distinctly uncertain.

I reach out and pat his cheek, relishing his soft, smooth scales under my palm. "I'm certain."

He bows, his head nearly reaching my pelvis, and then steps back. His huge wings extend out from behind him, so massive they make his body look small.

"When should I return?" he asks, his shadow fully encompassing me and most of the yard.

"It'll be a few weeks before we know if this worked," I say, feeling a pang in my chest at the idea I won't see him again for some time. But we've already gone this long only meeting once a month—I'll be fine. "I'll take the tests and keep you posted?"

He nods, and I can't read the expression on his dragon face. We exchange phone numbers, and then hiking his bag over his shoulder, Zakarion lifts off into the air. The gust of wind from his immense wings blows my hair into my face, but I still manage to wave as he lifts off and flies into the sky.

I'm going to need to hustle again.

But that's all right. I'm no stranger to the grind of keeping up with my basic living expenses and paying back school loans—not to mention the bill I racked up for the roof.

First thing the next morning, I sign up to be a driver, with the intention of carting partygoers from one place to another on weekend nights. Then I browse online job listings, where a freelance cleaning gig pops up.

Perfect. Some manual labor sounds like a good way to break up the tedium of waiting for the next pregnancy test.

Between cleaning jobs and chauffeuring, I still have time for some fall activities. I visit the pumpkin patch, then spend two nights cleaning and carving the pumpkins, though no trick-or-treaters ever come this far out of town. It's likely no one will even see them except Sarah and Jared, who come over one night to help me out with cutting silly faces into the pumpkins' corpses.

They're both mystified by my choice to help Zakarion outside of DreamTogether.

"He's... not paying you?" Sarah asks again, bafflement on her face, and I huff in exasperation.

"Yes, I told you that. I don't want him to pay me. He doesn't have any money now."

She's still perplexed. "What do you get out of it, then?" she asks. "You're basically donating your body. And you still have to work to pay all your bills."

I don't like to think of it that way, though. I'm donating the continuation of a dying species. Not to mention that getting fucked by Zakarion every few weeks isn't that big of an ask.

"It's just... it's the right thing to do," I finally answer. Maybe it won't satisfy her, but it's the best I've got.

Jared arches an eyebrow. "You have been sleeping with him for the last, I don't know, seven months?"

"So?" I ask. I can do basic math.

"*So*, that's a long time." He gives Sarah a Look, one of those couple things where they can talk to each other with their eyes.

"Do you think maybe you feel more for him than just... provider and client?" Sarah asks, picking up the torch where Jared left it.

I'm getting double-teamed.

"No," I say, at the same moment I think, *yes*. I feel quite a bit more for my mellow, commanding dragon, who also cares so much for my comfort and pleasure, than just *provider and client*. But I'm going to try to play it safe, even if it means lying to my friends. "Guys, I'm helping an endangered species. That's a worthy cause, isn't it?"

"Sure," Sarah says. "That's definitely the only reason you're doing this. Not so you can keep having mind-blowing sex or anything."

I cross my arms and pout, because I know nothing I say will dissuade them. And besides, they're not wrong.

"He's hundreds of years old," I say eventually. "Even if I

did feel anything for him, he's going to outlive me by... I don't know, centuries. Many of them." I'd looked it up online, and there were stories of dragons over a thousand years old who had only died recently. "It doesn't make sense to get attached to someone who will outlive you ten times over."

"Honey," Sarah says, patting my leg, "Might be a little late for that."

nine

ZAKARION

My head is light and fluffy as I fly home, and it remains that way when I lie down in my nest to sleep for the night. I dream of nothing but Sammy, her legs wrapped around me, her face smiling, her bouncy hair radiant around her head.

I decide to stay in the city, hoping I might hear from her soon, even if it's just an update. I know we don't *need* to see each other until her next ovulation cycle, but I hope she gives me an excuse to visit her sooner.

I wouldn't mind lounging in the grass with her on a nice fall afternoon, curled around her under the sun.

I was so dazed when I left Sammy's that I forget why I was avoiding my house in the city. Early the next morning, there's a rapping on my door.

Blinking wearily, I climb out of my nest. I'm still yawning as I open it, without considering who might be on the other side.

I'm greeted by an immense gryphon, with a razor-sharp beak and hard little eyes. Next to him—and rather lower to the ground—stands a woman in a sharp blazer, wearing sunglasses.

"Zakarion the dragon?" says the gryphon, and I recognize his voice.

Hell. It's the guy on the phone.

"Yes?" I ask, sounding tired to my own ears. "What can I do for you?"

"We're here to find out what else you know about Rodney's activities. What other priceless artifacts you've sold to him."

I scowl at her. "None." It's a blatant lie, but I don't think they'd be standing here asking me questions if they had proof of anything. They're trying to intimidate me, forgetting that I am a ten-foot-tall dragon.

The gryphon sighs and massages the bridge of his beak. "Look. We're not here to arrest you or anything. We're trying to get information about Rodney's trafficking operation so we can track down these valuables and return them to their rightful places."

"Trafficking?" I ask, baffled.

"Correct," says the woman. "Many of these are items of significant cultural and historical value. They should be back where they belong, where they came from."

I give her a blank look. "They came from my hoard," I snap.

"And what else do you have?" the woman presses. "What other stolen relics are you keeping in your *hoard*?"

"They are mine!" I bellow, enraged at the implication we have taken our treasures over the centuries by force. "Unless you have real business here, I'm going to ask you to leave."

The woman sniffs as she turns around to walk away, but the gryphon shakes his head at me.

"Maybe someday you'll understand," he says, then follows her back to their unmarked black car.

I'm still irritated over the visit from the two suits when I get a text message from Sammy a week later.

Negative.

She follows it up with a sad face.

My claws struggle with things like texting, so I pick up the phone and call her, instead. She answers with a surprised chirp.

"Hi!"

"Um, hi," I say smoothly. "Sorry. It's easier to call. It's only been a week, maybe try again in a few days?"

"I will," she says. There's a very... pregnant pause. "How are you, Zak?"

I blink. "Zak?"

"Do you mind me calling you that?"

No one's ever given me a nickname before. It's absolutely charming, while also being an atrocious choice.

"No, not at all. I like it." I smile as I tip the phone against the side of my head. "I'm... well." I choose not to tell her about my unexpected visitors. "Biding my time. And you?"

"Biding my time is a good way to put it." Sammy sighs. "Boring stuff. Driving. Some guy threw up in the back of my car last night, so I had a good time cleaning that up today."

I frown. "How much are you working?" This is what I liked about DreamTogether: I knew my human was cared for, that she was making a living wage without having to push herself. Now I have no such assurance, and in fact, she's doing the opposite.

Perhaps I should try again to find a different pawn shop. But I have a feeling she won't accept my money, and the last thing I need is for the gryphon and the grumpy woman to show up again.

"Why are you asking?" I can hear her voice tense up. "It's not that much. Just weekend nights, when everyone is partying."

That's good. Still, I wish I could take care of her, like before.

I try to remain neutral about it. "As long as it's not too stressful," I finally say.

"I'm used to dealing with people."

"I'm sure you're very good at it."

Sammy clears her throat. "Well, I'll call you the next time I take a test and let you know."

"Thank you," I tell her, earnestly. "For everything. For doing this with me."

"Of course." I can hear her bright smile in her voice, and wish I could see it for myself. "Maybe we should do some research in the meantime. Have any other dragons successfully had hatchlings recently?"

It's a wonderful question, and my eyebrows fly up high when she suggests something so obvious. "Oh, I think so. I connected with a few of them online last year." I don't mention that it was while I was searching for a partner.

"Can you ask them?" she says.

I nod affirmatively, but then realize she can't see it. "Yes, that's a great idea. I'll find out what I can." I want to ask then if she'd like to come and help. She would know all the right questions, I'm sure, and has the sunny disposition to get whatever she needs out of someone.

But before I can open my mouth, Sammy says, "Sounds good. I'll talk to you later, Zak."

I preen at the nickname. "You too, Sammy."

The call ends, and I hold the phone close to my chest, hoping I'll get to see her again soon.

SAMMY

It was tempting to ask Zakarion to come over and maybe give it another try. But it's not necessary, not at this stage. We should wait until right before I'm scheduled to ovulate again to maximize our potential.

Anyway, I don't have time now that I've picked up a tutoring job a few days a week. There's that bachelor's degree coming in handy.

I take another test a few days later, and call Zakarion again.

"Negative," I say. "I'm sorry."

"Don't be sorry." He pauses. "Actually, I've done some research, like you suggested, and contacted some other dragons who have successfully had hatchlings."

I perk up at this. "What did you find out?"

"Results... inconclusive. But I should have done this much sooner." He sighs wearily. "It turns out you were right —my body is too sensitive, and the conditions have to be just right for it to work." He pauses. "It's my fault."

"It's not anyone's fault," I say instantly. "It's just your biology." I wonder if this is why the dragon population has dwindled. What sort of environment do they need to successfully reproduce? "Did you learn anything about what might help? What sort of conditions you need?"

"Every couple I spoke with said it took a long time, and they tried in many different places. The one thing they all had in common was the full moon."

I furrow my brow. "The full moon? Really? But you're a dragon, not a werewolf."

Zak laughs a big, bellowing laugh on the other end. "The full moon is powerful, and doesn't just affect werewolves. It affects all cycles, apparently, including mine."

How odd. "So I ovulate, and you have a fertility time-frame, too? That will be tricky to line up. And no information about what location or weather might be best?"

"Sorry, no. We may have to experiment a little."

Instantly, my body heats at the idea. Oh no, I'll have to let him fuck me sideways until we get it right? Woe is me.

"That's okay," I say, in as comforting a way as I can. "We'll figure it out."

"Thank you." The emotion and sincerity in his voice takes me aback. "Thank you so much, Sammy. For doing this for me."

"For you and for all dragon-kind," I answer. But Zak doesn't say anything to that, and I have to check that the call hasn't been dropped. "Are you okay?"

"Fine," he says quickly. "Perhaps we can try again at your house, under the next full moon?"

I pull out my computer and bring up the lunar cycle. "I'm supposed to ovulate in two weeks," I say. "The full moon is in one week, though. Should we try anyway?"

"Yes!" Zak says immediately. "I mean, I think that's a good idea."

I have to smile. I'm glad that he's eager to see me again,

as eager as I am to see him. I know I need to curb that feeling, but it still makes me tingle.

"Great. Then let's meet at my house, next Friday evening."

"Sounds good." There's another pause. "I hope you take care of yourself between now and then."

"Don't worry. I'm sticking to my exercise routine and the nutrition recommendations that DreamTogether gave me—"

"Not like that," he interrupts. "Emotionally speaking. I worry about you trying to make ends meet. I want to help, however I can."

That puts a smile on my face. "I'll be fine. I promise. I won't overwork myself."

"Thank you." He lets out a breath of relief. "I'll see you soon."

We say goodbye and hang up, and I just hope Friday comes quickly.

ZAKARION

She's doing it for the good of my species, not because she likes me. And that's... that's fine. That's good, even. It's like we agreed: no emotional attachment.

It still hurt, though Sammy did nothing wrong.

When I'm not hunting to keep up my strength, I spend the afternoons soaking in the remaining autumn sunlight and warming my body, hoping it will help on Friday night. I worry endlessly about how much Sammy is working, if her defensive tone was any indication. I want to pay her, even just supplement her income so she doesn't have to push so hard, but I keep thinking about what that gryphon said.

Is my hoard really not... mine?

By the time our meeting day rolls around, I'm so pent up that my cocks keep extruding from my slit when I so much as think about Sammy, or her bouncing breasts, or her big, curly hair. But I carefully don't attend to my needs, turning my mind to less appealing things like stinky, old meat, so I can save all of it for her.

No, wait. *For my future hatchling.* That's why we're doing this—to get me the thing I've wanted most. And how sweet it will be, to lie curled around my small offspring, teaching them all the ways that my parents taught me. Ancient secrets, and words of wisdom, and another chance for my kind to go on into the future, as uncertain as it might be.

When it's finally time, I launch into the sky and make my way to Sammy's house. Her beat-up vehicle isn't there when I land in the yard, so I lie down in the grass and wait for her.

Soon, she pulls up and hops out. Her dark eyes are big, and her smile is wide and radiant.

"Zak!" I stand up as she jogs over to me, and she looks like she's about to throw her arms around me when she stops a few feet away. She seems to remember herself then, and claps her hands in front of her instead. "You beat me back. It's nice to see you."

"It's wonderful to see you," I say, realizing too late that I should probably tone it back, too. But her face brightens even more, and I subconsciously preen, my neck rising up and curling to show off my wings.

"Do you want dinner?" she asks. "It'll be a while until sundown."

I should probably tell her that I've already eaten all of

my week's sustenance, but I'm eager to spend more time with her, so I agree to dinner.

She cooks up a pair of steaks she bought, and prepares them with some vegetables that will taste awful, but I'll tolerate for her. Dragons don't need anything besides red meat, and in fact, I don't think my body can process what she's making. But I know it will make her happy to eat together, so I sit down on the floor in her kitchen as she serves the food.

She has a cute little house, but I have to make sure I stay down on all fours because the ceiling isn't quite high enough for my long neck. Sammy apologizes quite a few times, until I assure her that I'm fine and even my own caves have low points, so I'm used to it. I'm just happy enjoying her personal sunshine.

After we eat, we sit in the backyard on a blanket and wait for the sun to fully set. The brilliant orange light bathes Sammy's face like liquid gold. I think again of how much it bothers me that she left such a good job at DreamTogether for my hatchling, and I have no way to repay her.

"Sammy," I finally say. "I want you to know how much this means to me. I wish I could compensate you—"

"We've talked about this, haven't we, Zak?" she says in a chiding tone. "You don't need to."

"—I know, but I want to help, in any way I can." I furrow my brow, wishing she could understand just how deeply I feel the need to provide for her, to make her life easier. "I hope that you'll call on me any time you need me."

She gives me a wide, affectionate, sincere smile. "Thank you. Your gratitude is all I need. I'm happy to be doing something that matters, you know? I've always wanted that. I tried to get a degree that would help people, but..." Sammy flops back on the blanket and rests her head on her hands like a pillow. "That dream was too big for me. I want to make change still, but in small ways. That's why I live out here." She gestures at her big yard. "Nobody else wanted this dingy old house, so I bought it. I wanted to make it nicer, to clean up the land, plant some native plants. Try to live in ways that will leave the smallest footprint possible."

I open my mouth to tell her, *if that is what you like, perhaps you should try my mountain*, but that would be far too bold. No, from everything I've gathered, Sammy enjoys her life here. I'm simply glad that her generous, kind heart has chosen to help me.

"It's become a very beautiful place," I tell her, meaning every word of it. She has clearly taken a dull stone and polished it into a gem here.

"Aw, thank you." Sammy adjusts like she's going to lean against me, but stops herself.

"I think you change everything you touch," I tell her. "You take light around with you."

Her head tilts so she's gazing up at me, her mouth round. "You know how to compliment a girl," she says with a giggle.

I know that she's trying to diffuse my compliments, and perhaps she's right to. But I mean all of them. Just Sammy's existence changes the world, a little at a time.

As the moon rises, we sit closer and closer together. Her sweet smell fills up my head, and soon my cocks are ready to slide out of me, to find their way inside her again to that warm, perfect place where they belong.

I wonder what it would be like to fit both of them inside her. As soon as the thought appears, I banish it, because mating that way serves no purpose for procreation. It would be purely for my gratification—well, and hopefully hers, too.

But maybe she would be more open to it than I expect. Sammy is the sort of woman who enjoys herself, who wants to make this pleasurable for both of us. I will have to broach it in the future, should this not work tonight.

When the full moon has risen, it bathes the world in a silver glow. Sammy moves next to me, and when I glance over I find her shedding her shirt and bra. I'm filled with gratification that she wants me to take her naked. It feels much less like a transaction that way.

My slit parts as my cocks both peek their heads out, wanting a good look at her, too. As she wiggles off her pants, they fully extrude, the tips already leaking for her.

"Which one?" she asks, walking to where I sit in the grass, unable to hide just how horny I am for her.

I blink down at my twin cocks, then back up at her. "Whichever you prefer."

She waggles her eyebrows as she takes my upper cock in her hand. I jerk immediately because the sensation is so intense. I've been holding off for too long, I guess. If I'm not careful...

"Wait," I say, holding her hand in mine. Sammy wilts under me.

"What is it?" she asks. "Did I do something wrong?"

I shake my head rapidly. "No, no. The opposite. I'm going to go off way too soon." I have to take a few long, deep breaths to collect myself.

"Oh, well then." Sammy's smile turns wild and wicked. She steps closer, and rises up onto her toes so she can slide her arms around my neck. With her this near, her soft skin rubbing across my scales, my cocks are even harder, even hungrier to be inside her.

"Are you ready?" she asks me.

"Ready?" I echo, not sure what she intends. Then she puts her weight on my neck, lifts up one leg, and positions herself over me. My mouth falls open as she guides herself down onto the sloped head of my upper cock, and just the sensation of her wet outer lips sends a shiver right into my testicles.

Oh, hell. I'm not going to be able to hold back.

Sammy whimpers as she lowers her body, bringing me inside her. I can feel the softly-ribbed texture of her channel against the nubs of my cock as she sinks down, and I can't help wrapping my arms around her, holding onto her tight as she soaks up most of me on her first stroke.

"Sammy," I murmur, dragging my claws over her soft curls. "You feel amazing."

"So do you." Her voice comes out choked, and when I look down, I find her mouth open in bliss as she lifts herself up, and then swallows me up a second time. My other hand curls under her ass to help her, where my lower cock is drooling all over her, and she moans again as we start to work together. Over and over, I lift her up and then slide her down on my cock, as far as she can take it.

Meanwhile, my lower cock drags along beneath her, and I keep picturing how it would feel to put both of them inside her, to take her fully and completely. My eyes roll back in my head, and as Sammy swallows me up to my swell, I can't hold back anymore.

It hits me hard. "I'm sorry," I groan as my hips buck, and the absolute bliss of her strikes me like a hammer. Shit, maybe I should have taken care of my needs at least once in the interim.

My whole body tenses and I thrust inside her, hard, releasing everything. Sammy shouts in surprise as I shoot jet after jet of my hot seed into her, drenching her before I'm even all the way inside her body. She moans prettily as I tremble, and thick, white fluid spills out of her, dribbling down her thighs and onto my lower cock.

Sammy grins a huge, mischievous grin. "That good, huh?" she asks, getting her feet under her again. But it's humiliating I couldn't even get her to her finish first.

So I take her by the hips, and she squeaks as I urge her to the ground.

"Lie down," I say in a rather commanding tone. Her eyes widen, and then she obeys, sitting down on the blanket before falling back onto it. I pull her legs apart and flick my tongue out to taste the air. Our scents mixed together smells absolutely exquisite. "The longer you're on your back, the better chance all my seed will stay inside you," I say, by way of explanation. It's a silly excuse, but I need one right now for the very intimate—and unnecessary—activity I'm about to engage in.

I extend my long neck down so my snout is between her thighs, and Sammy's head jerks up. "What are you going to do?" she asks.

"I'm going to lick you," I tell her, pushing her legs even further apart. My tongue darts out and sweeps over her slit, which is lovely and open for me. Sammy lets out a gasp as I taste her. Her anatomy is quite interesting, and now, perhaps, I can experiment a little. I've always wanted to do it, but it was never toward the purpose of mating, so I never tried before at DreamTogether.

But now, with our new freedom, I'm going to try everything, even if I have to make up an excuse each step of the way.

ten

SAMMY

OH, WOW. ZAKARION'S TONGUE FEELS LIKE NOTHING ELSE IN the world. It's long and thick and forked at the tip, and black, too, which sends a shock of surprise through me when he extends the whole thing and brushes it over my clit.

"Mmmm." My head falls back on the blanket as he does it again, then again. "Right there. That's amazing."

Obediently Zakarion continues taunting my clit, circling it and pressing it down and flicking it from side to side. Then he dips down, sampling further into my pussy before returning to his attack. I'm riding higher and higher, heading into the moon high up above us, and I find my hands sliding up the scales of his head to the two horns above it. They're easy to hold onto, and instinctually I grab them as he works faster and faster with that amazing tongue.

"Yes," I manage. "Yes, please, Zak."

He groans when I use the name and eats me harder, until finally I explode. I cry out as it blasts through me, and my hips snap up into his snout. His claws tighten in my flesh, holding me down to earth as I orgasm so hard my vision turns momentarily white.

When I've finally opened my eyes again, I find my dragon crouched above me, his two cocks gloriously hard. Just seeing them, imagining what it would be like to take all of him at once, I'm ready for more.

"Zak," I say, sitting up so I can gently wrap my hands around his lower cock. "Do you think it would be possible at some point to... use both of them?"

He squints and tilts his head. "Both? At the same time?" He gives me an uncertain look, and I think maybe I was an idiot for asking. Of course he doesn't want to use the other one *there*.

"Never mind," I say, flapping a hand. "It's silly. We're not here for that."

He stops me by taking my hand in his, his massive claws dwarfing me. "No, no. It's not silly at all. I think..." Zak swallows, his long neck bobbing. "...I would like that. Very much." Then he sighs. "Maybe too much."

"Too much?" I laugh at him. "It's sex. You're supposed to enjoy it."

"And I do." He looks very serious. "I enjoy it immensely with you."

Oh. My smile falls. Now I understand what he's saying. He doesn't want to encourage that kind of bonding. It's antithetical to what we're doing, and what we agreed on.

"I see." I pull my thighs closed, which are still sticky with him. "I get it. We won't do that, then."

Zak frowns, so I try to distract us by stroking his lower cock, which is full and hard already. He has more to give me, and this is our best chance tonight.

"Why don't we use this one this time?" I ask, scooting closer. Still fisting him, I rub his upper cock against my belly.

Zak lets out a muffled groan, and his huge wings lift up behind him. He nods quickly, and with his gaze intent, focuses on kneeling between my thighs. One of his big claws slips under my hips to lift me, positioning me perfectly for his lower cock to slip inside.

Oh, the sensation of those nubs pressing into me is heaven. I'm still swollen up from my orgasm, but Zak moves slow like he always does, giving me a little before retreating, then offering more while his upper cock drags over my clit.

So I let him, as frustrating as it is to take him slowly. I know it will make it all the more delightful later.

His gaze is riveted on where our bodies are connected. "I much prefer this method of mating to the table at DreamTogether," he says hoarsely, his reptilian, yellow eyes traveling up to mine. He reaches out with one claw and, more gently than I would think is possible, cups my breast in one of his huge hands. He groans as he settles further inside me, thrusting shallowly a few times to taunt me with his knobbed cock before returning to his place. I'm loosening up, getting wetter and wetter as he continues teasing me, and soon all I want is that massive swell to fit into me.

"Please, Zak," I say, arching my hips up to take even more of him. His eyelids droop as he seizes one of my legs, rooting me to him.

"You want more?" he asks, a feral grin revealing all of his white fangs.

I nod rapidly, and with a grunt, he gives it to me. That swell pushes in, and I'm so open to him that it squeezes into me, fitting right where it belongs.

"Oh, Sammy." All of Zakarion's dominance drains away at once, and his brows tilt in a shy kind of affection. "You're so beautiful."

I open my mouth to reply, to tell him just how lovely I

find him, but then he fucks that swell in even deeper and I cry out instead. He pins down my arms with one claw and holds my hips up with the other, and starts thrusting with abandon. Every time that wonderful, textured cock slips in and out of me, I crawl closer and closer to that same place up in the clouds where all my pleasure is hidden away.

"Zak!" I scream it as he shoves himself deep inside me, withdrawing only enough that the swell is free, and then pushes me open with it again. Over and over he torments me this way, those intense eyes with the long pupils staring down into me with every furious thrust of his hips. Smoke rises from his nostrils, and the faster he moves, the more of it pours out.

"Sammy," he growls, now gripping one of my thighs while he uses me like a doll, "I'm going to plant my hatchling in you, tonight. Right now."

"Please!" I call out to him. "Please, Zak. Fill my belly with your hatchling."

These must be magic words, because his eyes roll back and he snarls. Then, head tilted up, nose pointed toward the moon... he releases a jet of pure flame into the night sky.

Now, Zakarion is fucking me with a feral intensity that hasn't emerged before, burying his cock as deep as he can before yanking it back out again. With every single raw thrust, his upper cock pressing into my clit, I'm screaming. Before long, I go roaring over my finish line. He strikes again and again, howling something incomprehensible. Every pump of his cock through me, those nubs rubbing all along me, catapults me higher and higher.

Zakarion lets out another immense bellow of flame, and with a roar, he unleashes. The volume of his come is so immense that it fills me utterly full, so full that I wail and squeeze and he shivers and trembles in return, and there's a wet sound as it's expelled from me. Even more of it shoots out of his upper cock, painting my tits and my belly, even landing as far up as my chin.

When Zak has collapsed to his forelegs, holding himself up over me while remaining buried in my pussy, I run my finger through the puddle on my collarbone.

"If that doesn't work," I say lightly, chuckling, "I don't know what will."

Zak flashes me a smile in return, and I resist the urge to lean up and kiss his snout. He's perfect, really—the best lover I've ever had by miles.

I will genuinely be sad when this works.

ZAKARION

I remain lodged inside Sammy for some time, just enjoying the feel of her even as my cocks start to recede. Finally, I pull free, and they both retreat back into my body.

"That's so neat," she says as I help her to her feet. My seed drips down her thighs in an extremely lovely way. "I'll never get tired of how cool it is."

I'm proud that she finds me interesting and attractive. It's as if she truly sees me—my body and what's inside it.

We spend another hour lying together in the grass, just talking. It's easy to lose myself in conversation with her.

"How old are you?" she asks. Then she bites her lip. "Sorry if that was an insensitive question."

I shake my head. "Not at all. Nearly three hundred, in another two years."

"So you've been around for every major modern event?"

She strokes her chin thoughtfully. My tail has wrapped itself around her ankle of its own accord, but she doesn't seem to mind.

"It depends on what you mean by 'modern,' but for the most part, yes. That doesn't mean much, though. I have spent most of my life at my mountain. Dragons generally do not participate in the world's activities."

She nods in understanding. "You keep to yourselves."

"Yes. Though we will venture out in times of peace to explore, to discover new things." I sigh. "I only went on one tour myself. Typically, dragons go on a tour to visit their kinfolk around the world, during which time we would seek out partners. But all the dragons my parents knew were dead, so I had no one to visit."

Sammy's mouth tilts down on both sides. "What? All dead? Oh, Zak. That's terrible."

I wistfully shake my head. "It is how it is. Luckily, since then I have had a chance to connect with others, thanks to the internet." I laugh. "One of those modern conveniences I have come to appreciate."

Next to me, I sense Sammy shivering. She is naked out here, after all, so I pull her in closer to my chest, where I make my fire.

"Oh, wow!" Her eyes fly wide. "You're so warm!"

I chuckle. "I am a dragon."

She smiles brightly as she curls in tighter, and her eyes close in pleasure. "That's so nice. My personal heater." As I laugh again, she giggles. "Your whole body rumbles when you do that," she says.

It's when I pull a curl away from her face and try to tuck it behind her ear, but it springs free, that I realize I love her.

Reflexively, I release her, and all my muscles tense. I'm not supposed to feel this way, certainly about a human I barely know. But the sensation of it is so powerful, I know the truth immediately.

Sammy furrows her brow. "Are you okay, Zak?" she asks.

"I..." I don't know what to say. She was very clear with me about the terms of this. I have to nip this in the bud, so my feelings can't grow any stronger. Cuddling with her in her front yard will not help towards that end. "I should go," I finally tell her.

All the joy falls from Sammy's face. "Oh." Her eyes drop down to the ground. "Okay. Yeah. I guess that's good."

She gets up quickly and puts her clothes back on. It's clear that I've hurt her, which is not what I wanted to do. I'm only trying to respect her wishes and her boundaries, and now I wish I could take those words back.

I rise up onto two feet and set a hand on her shoulder. "I'm sorry, Sammy."

When she turns around, she has that familiar bright, fake smile on her face. "I understand. This is the right thing to do. Thank you for showing me such a nice time tonight."

Her mask is back on. My cocks shrivel inside me.

"O-of course," I say, hesitant. "I could say the same for you."

"I'll call you when I take a test next week, okay?" Her voice is cheery, and strangely hard.

I nod slowly, then turn away. "All right," I agree. If she has put on her *professional* face, then there is little more for us to say.

Without a further goodbye—I don't want to drive the knife even deeper into my own chest—I extend my wings and flap, taking off into the sky.

But leaving her feels heavy, and I wish I hadn't said anything at all.

I fly home slowly, making lazy circles through the air, trying to remember how wonderful it was to make love to Sammy and not how miserable it feels now.

Already, I miss her. I hated seeing that fake smile on her face, the one that doesn't reach her eyes, and wish that we could go back to lying on the blanket, talking about our lives.

I try to remember that we've been very intimate as a part of this process, and how I feel about her is driven by an instinctual need to bond. It's not real. She's human, small, and fragile. She wants a human partner someday, maybe children to play on those ancient swings.

I am not the fulfillment she's looking for, and she's not that for me, either. She will only live another sixty, perhaps seventy years, while I would go on for many more centuries after that.

Or worse, I would follow her into the darkness beyond as my father followed my mother, leaving our hatchlings alone as I was.

When I return to my house in the city, I don't keep up with my eating, choosing instead to sleep as a means of passing the time. A week goes by in a flash, even though my stomach is grumbling whenever I open my eyes. I think it's a Friday when my phone rings.

It's Sammy.

I answer quickly. "Hi, how are you?"

She hesitates before answering. "I'm fine, thank you!" she says, with that fake sunny tone. "Bad news, though. Negative."

I sigh. Perhaps this is truly all a pointless effort.

"But I'll test again next week, and if it's still negative, we can meet up on the full moon again!" She sounds so optimistic.

"Sammy," I begin. We should stop doing this, before my feelings for her grow even more. If we haven't succeeded yet, surely it wasn't meant to be.

"Perhaps we should try somewhere else," she barrels on. "You said the other dragons who conceived were able to do it at home? That might be the answer."

I bite back what I was about to say, that we should quit now and give up. She's right. "I suppose we could do it at my house," I say. I could bring her into my big nest of pillows when I put one of my cocks in her. She would probably like that.

"Is that where you live? A house?" She hums. "Is that where your hoard is?"

"No, that's at my mountain." The mountain is my true home, really. "It's far away."

"And how long have you lived there?"

I wonder where she's going with this. "All my life," I say cautiously. "I was born there."

"Ding ding ding!" she cries into the phone, and I have to pull it away from the side of my head to protect my hearing. "That's the place we're supposed to do it, Zak! Obviously!"

"Obviously?" I ask, perplexed.

"Duh! That's your *home*. It's where you're likely to be most comfortable, with ideal temperature and humidity. If your parents were able to reproduce there, then you should be able to, as well."

"Oh," I say stupidly. She has a very valid point.

Sammy squeals. "I think we solved it! If we have sex at your mountain, under the full moon, I bet it'll work."

I can't believe the thought never even crossed my mind. I've been too distracted by my emotions lately. But if she comes to my mountain, she'll see my hoard—everything my ancestors have collected over the years. My most intimate place.

My heart stutters at the idea of what it would mean to me to share that with her, to show her my history.

"When is the next full moon?" I ask.

"Three weeks."

Damn. That's a long way off, and I can't think of an excuse to see her before then, so instead I say, "Shall we meet then?"

"Yes, of course! Where is it? Should I drive?"

I snort into the phone, which causes the screen to fog up from the steam. "No, no. I'll carry you there. No car can reach my mountain."

She giggles. "Sounds cool. Okay. Then I'll see you in three weeks."

I nod vigorously. "See you in three weeks."

eleven

ZAKARION

WHEN I FLY BACK TO MY MOUNTAIN, I FACE A WHIRLWIND OF cleaning. It's been more than a hundred years since I gave this place a decent once-over, and there are many tunnels, some clogged with truly embarrassing things—a few deer bones, shed scales, and dirt I've dragged in with me. I sweep every last crevice, even ones I doubt Sammy will see, and dust off everything in the Museum.

I'm definitely going to show her the Museum.

I want to impress Sammy with my mountain home, though I couldn't say why. It's not as if she would live here with me while she's carrying my hatchling. That does sound lovely, and I think she would like how remote it is.

Though perhaps she wouldn't like not having her car.

Still, none of these are things I can entertain. As much as I would love to hunt for her, to cook her fresh meat covered in herbs and roasted by my fire, that's not what this is. It would be foolish of me to get attached to a human, only to watch her age and die.

Trying not to think of such sad things, I address my hoard. It's also a mess, and I clean almost everything, sure to remove any bones and remnants of my laziness. I move my nicest jewels to the top of the hoard, and pat it when I'm done.

At last, it's time to bring Sammy here.

I fly quickly back to the city, excited to see her again after so much time apart. But if this works, as she suspects it will, this may be the last time I see her for some time—and the last time I get to enjoy her wonderful body.

I hope she will be amenable to my suggestion that we continue to meet regularly so I can check on the hatchling's growth and her well-being. I want to provide what I can for her, whether it's simply emotional support. I owe her far, far more than that, but I don't know what else I can offer her.

When I land on Sammy's front lawn, the weather is chillier than the last time I was here. Fall is in full swing, and the trees are starting to change color. It's beautiful at her home with the yellow autumn leaves all about, and I breathe in the smell before walking to her front door to knock.

Before I can tap it once with my knuckle, the door flies open, and Sammy is standing there with her plump cheeks and bright eyes.

Most unexpectedly, she throws her arms around me, hands winding up my neck. I catch her, and squeeze her back, pleased to have her body so close to mine again. This time I did not make the mistake of leaving my needs unat-tended. Every time I thought of her, my cocks extruded and I took care of business, and still generated plenty of seed. I should have no trouble planting a hatchling in her tonight if her guess about the location of my mountain is correct.

"Sorry," Sammy says, extricating herself from me. She quickly backs away, putting space between us. "I'm just happy to see you."

I offer her a big smile. "No need to apologize. I'm pleased to see you again, as well."

Rather than smiling in return, she frowns, and I wonder if I've said something wrong.

"Shall we?" she asks in a more neutral tone. Right. Emotional distance. She wants to be wary of crossing lines, and we likely already crossed one just now.

I nod. "Can I carry you? On my back? That will be easiest, I think."

This time she does grin widely. "I was so hoping you'd suggest that."

I stoop down low so she can climb on, and I scoop her up by her behind so I can heft her onto my shoulders more comfortably. She clings onto my neck, and though I can't see her face, I can imagine her surprise as my wings flap and I lift off into the air.

It's much harder to fly with the extra weight, but I'm able to do it. She shrieks as we rise high above her house, and I worry she's frightened of heights.

"Amazing!" she cries. "It's beautiful up here!"

I'm elated that she likes it.

"Wait until you see my home," I tell her, and I start off in the direction of my mountain.

SAMMY

We fly and fly, heading north, and I wish I'd brought more than just a sweater. It's frigid up here at this altitude, and I have to lean down close to Zakarion and wrap my arms around his neck just to stay close to his body. He's so warm underneath me, his scales smooth and strangely soft, that I just want to hold onto him forever.

I watch the country become city, and then the city fades into the suburbs, until we're passing over wide patches of farmland. Even that eventually gives way to vast wilderness, open meadows and dense trees.

We're flying over a mountain range, and I'm getting sleepy when I hear Zak finally say, "We're here."

I sit up as he starts to descend, winding downward in circles like a bird of prey. Below us is a massive peak, higher than all the neighboring ones by a long shot. There's snow decorating the exposed rock like icing on a cake. Zak flaps a few more times before there's a loud *thump*, and I peek over his shoulder to find us standing on a high, high ledge.

I squeak and cling onto him tighter when I see how close we are to the cliffside, and how far down I could fall if I took one wrong step. Zakarion chuckles, and puts his hands underneath me to keep me on his shoulders. His wings retract, folding up along his back to either side of me, and then he steps into shadow.

A torch is lit on the closest wall, revealing a long, stone tunnel. Once we're safely inside and no longer standing on the exposed rock face, I whisper in his ear, "I think I can walk now."

Zak nods and helps me down off his back, setting me down neatly on the floor. It is, bizarrely, much warmer in here than outside, when it should be just as cold.

"Where's that heat coming from?" I ask.

Zakarion tilts his head down and smirks. "There is hot water running throughout the mountain. We have diverted it to keep all of the halls and rooms warm." He stoops down and puts an arm around my shoulders. "Come. I have much to show you."

I'm disappointed when he steps away again and leads me down the hall. We pass more torches, and then as the hall curves, a great space opens up ahead of us.

It's gold. The whole room is pure, shining gold. Torches reflect off of the surface of piles and piles of objects, most of them glimmering yellow but some silver, and the light bounces every which way to illuminate the walls.

I can't even utter a "wow." My voice is caught in my throat as I take in the sprawling space, filled with a pile of jewels and riches of all kinds. It's a veritable sea of ancient beauty.

"This is amazing," I finally say, taking another step inside. Zakarion is watching with a wide grin on his face, showing every last one of his huge fangs. "This is yours? What you've collected over the years?"

"Oh, not just mine," he says, reaching down to pick up a ring lying in the middle of the floor. He blows on it, then rubs it against his chest before tossing it into the pile. "My parents contributed, and my mother's parents before her, and... well, you get the idea."

Many millennia of wealth, all gathered here. I can't fathom how much it's worth.

"Do all dragons have hoards like yours?" I ask.

"I don't really know. I haven't interacted with many others of my kind."

I'm baffled by it. "But with all this, you couldn't afford DreamTogether anymore?"

Zak's shoulders curl up to his neck. "Well..." he begins,

casting a worried look around the room, anywhere but me. "There was this imp. He was my connection. Then, somehow, he was discovered selling something of mine, and now..." He gazes mournfully down at his hoard. "I cannot sell anything else. I've even been told that all of this—" He gestures around the room. "—isn't mine. That I should return it to where it came from."

I frown. "Who told you this?"

"The government." He scratches his nose. "Something about items of cultural significance?"

Oh. Then it dawns on me. What he has here truly are remnants of another time, beautiful and important artifacts that tell the history of many places and people.

I kneel down and pick up a small gold crown.

"Belonged to a prince," Zakarion says, nodding at it. "I believe from the year 1230."

Turning it over in my hands, I wonder who that prince was. "Do you know the history of everything here?" I ask, returning it gently to the pile when I see how protectively he's hovering over me.

"Of course." He arches an eyebrow. "Don't you know the origin of everything in your home?"

"Yes, but I don't own as much as you do."

Zakarion looks out over his hoard. "But every piece is valuable, every piece has a memory. It's up to me to retain those memories, to preserve the history of my father and mother and their parents before them."

I follow his gaze. "And each of them has their own history, too. I wonder how much scholars could learn just from this one crown?"

Zakarion blinks like he never even thought about it.

"Hmm." He scratches his chin. Then, with a brief shake of his head, he gestures with one hand for me to follow him.

"There's much more to see, and we don't have a lot of time until the sun is fully down."

Right. We're here for a reason.

Zak leads me out of his treasure room to another hall-way, which descends downward at a steady pace. It grows narrower as we pass, and I want to reach out and hold onto his tail in case we get separated down here.

Then we emerge into another room, not as large as the last one, with lower ceilings. Wooden cases with glass faces rim the walls. Zakarion retrieves a torch and carries it to the first case, the flame shining across the display.

"What is this place?" I ask as Zak hands me another torch. I almost drop it because I've never held fire on a stick this close to my face before.

"The Museum." Inside the case rests a curl of stone with a snake's head at the tip. "This is Medusa's hair," he says.

I gasp. "Medusa's actual hair?"

Zak just nods, and I have no reason not to believe him.

He shows me everything in the Museum, all sorts of trea-sures dating back thousands of years. There's so much history, so many pieces of time preserved here.

"Did your parents acquire these?" I ask.

He nods toward a painting on the opposite wall. "My mother purchased that before she died," he says. "She appreciated art, and met the painter personally."

"I'm so sorry about your mother," I say. "What happened to her? If I can ask?"

Zakarion's eyes wander away from mine and travel aimlessly upward, as if he is remembering something long past.

"A disease," he finally says. "It is what took many of the dragons of her age, when we were already few and far between. It stained her scales gray, until finally it took her life."

Zakarion's shoulders curl forward, and I reach out to stroke his back. "I'm so sorry."

He shakes his head. "I have had time to grieve, and my pain is much smaller now than it used to be. But it's still there. Losing her was miserable, but when my father grew heartsick..." He closes his eyes. "It wasn't long after that when he passed away, too. As is the way with dragons."

I stare at him. "That's common?"

He nods, clearly lost in his memories. "Yes. Dragons bond deeply, in our souls. When one of the pair dies, the other typically follows soon after."

The steady thrum of my heartbeat speeds up, growing louder in my ears. Now I know with complete certainty that what I feel for Zakarion is doomed. There can never be anything between us. If ever he reciprocated, if we tried to have a relationship beyond this hatchling, I would be sentencing him to an early death.

A shudder runs down my back. I couldn't do that to him. Not ever.

I'm quieter as he shows me the rest of his collection, then Zakarion treks on to a series of smaller rooms. As we walk and explore, I try to push the ugly thought out of my mind. We have an agreement for just this reason. Avoiding a romantic entanglement is simpler, and much safer for Zak.

The rooms down below are cozy, and they must be his living quarters. The main room has a fire pit and a hole carved into the ceiling that brings in fresh light. An adjoining room is full of animal pelts and embroidered throw pillows. Here, Zak clears his throat, then pulls the curtain closed over the room again after showing it to me.

Oh. That must be his bedroom. It looks so warm and

soft, I'm disappointed when we walk away. As we return the way we came, I can't help but think about how comfortable and lovely that big nest would be to sleep in.

Soon, though, we emerge into the treasure room again. I can see outside the cave from here, and the evening light is quickly fading, leaving a periwinkle horizon in its wake.

Zakarion walks up beside me, and ever-so-slightly brushes his claws over my hip.

"Are you ready?" he asks, bringing his long neck down so his snout is very close to my ear. "After tonight, you'll be growing my hatchling inside you." His hand lands on my back and curls around my hip, until his palm is up against my belly. I'm wracked by a full-body shiver.

"Yes." My breath is already coming faster as his hand splays out across my stomach, and he shifts himself to stand directly behind me. "It will grow right here." I cover his huge hand with my tiny one. His other hand cups one of my breasts, and then he slides a claw over the tip of a nipple, through my shirt. I gasp as he ducks lower, tracing his hand down toward my ass, his hot breath brushing the shell of my ear.

"And which cock will be so lucky," he says in a low, rumbling voice, "as to plant it?"

I imagine both of those thick, swollen things inside me, and a gasp escapes my lips. My hips roll back of their own accord, so my ass is pressed up against his belly.

He huffs into my ear again. "Take off your pants." I'm so surprised by the command in his voice that it takes a moment for my fingers to obey, plucking open the buttons of my jeans. He hooks a claw in the band and helps me pull them down, along with my shoes and underwear. Soon I'm standing naked in front of him, and both of his cocks are now unsheathed, visibly swollen and spilling over.

Zakarion reaches underneath me and scoops me up by the butt. I squeak and grip tight around his neck, which makes him let out that deep, rumbling sound of pleasure.

"I think I will take you with one at a time," he says, the tips of his claws digging into my ass. "And let both of them have a taste of you."

twelve

ZAKARION

If this is the last time I get to take her this way, then I
want to enjoy it as much as I possibly can.

My Sammy is already dripping for me when I lift her,
and my tongue flicks out to taste how good she smells.
Guiding her by the hips, I line her up carefully with my
upper cock, and simply dip inside her.

"Don't tease me forever," she whines, and I have to laugh.
I do like to take my time with her, and make sure her small
body is ready for me. But that isn't what she wants. Not
tonight.

I wonder if she's been practicing for how well and readily
she accepts me. As the knobbed head of my cock slips inside
her, she buckles forward, winding her arms even tighter
around my neck.

"Zakarion," she murmurs as I lift her up, then slide her
back down again until I'm almost halfway seated. "You feel
fucking amazing."

My wings lift off my back at the praise, the ridges along

my back rising up. It's as if I was made for her, designed to fit inside her, the way she conforms to my shape. She sucks me in and holds me there until I lift her again, her infinitesimal weight easily gliding up and down. I slide into her again until my swell is widening her for me, and her cunt gives so easily to it.

"Your body is perfect," I tell her, as both my cocks throb. "Made just right for me." I lower my neck, curling it down over her shoulder as I drop her lower. She nods her head rapidly, squeezing me while also allowing me even deeper in.

And then, I'm there, my swell fitting perfectly inside her body, her heat pulsing around me in time with the rapid beating of her heart. I have to suck in a breath and hold it just to keep myself in check.

I still have much more to do before I go off.

With a few more deep, experimental thrusts, I pull my first cock out of her, much to Sammy's displeasure. But before she can speak her objection, I sling my wet upper cock across her mound, and fit the head of my lower cock into her dripping channel. She gapes down, her breath held, as I slide back in where I belong.

My toes practically curl at the wash of sensation. Sammy cries out as I sink in deep, then I lift her up until we almost separate. I rub my cheek along her soft hair, simply relishing the way she brings me into her small body. Then I drop her again, and she cries out my name.

Being the devil she is, Sammy lowers one hand to the cock that's splayed up along her clit, all the way to her belly. She strokes it, pushing it down to get friction, and the sensation of both my cocks receiving attention at the same time almost makes me erupt.

"Sammy," I moan, driving into her with abandon. She's

pumping me now, panting each time I thrust into her, crying out whenever she sinks all the way down. I feel my fire starting to build, as hard as I'm trying to keep it tamped down. My wings extend, and before I know what I'm doing, I have my arms clasping Sammy tightly against me as I flap once, twice, and launch us into the air.

She shrieks, and her arms clamp tight around me—and so does her cunt. I groan, then flap again, bringing us higher into the sky. I'm fucking her faster, my wings moving in time with my hips, and she's crying out with every wild thrust.

"Zak!" Sammy is gripping my neck even tighter. "Oh, fuck, that's so good, please don't drop me—"

"I will never drop you," I murmur to her, rising higher and higher into the air, the moon hovering far above us like an immense silver coin. I clutch Sammy close as I fuck her, and the sheer bliss of being inside her almost ends me. But I need to hold out, just a little longer.

"Zak, oh, please, oh," Sammy's calls are disjointed and desperate. "Oh, just like that, yes, please!"

I repeat the motion with laser precision, finding exactly what pleases her and pinpointing it, trying to stay concentrated even though her marvelous hair is bathed in white from the moon, and her long, dark eyelashes are dusted with silver. The whole world is spread out beneath us and her cries are filling the sky like perfect, heavenly music. I bounce her faster, slamming into her, and finally... her mouth falls open, and her cries stop.

Oh, nothing has ever felt so good as my Sammy gripping me like iron as her climax takes over. She's so wet and so tight that as I frantically fuck her through it, my own reserve of self-control crumbles at last.

I thrust into her once more, and tilt my head back as

flames erupt from my mouth. My seed spurts out, shooting across her belly, filling her up as my hips jerk once, and then again, and still there's more coming. I moan as Sammy's tiny body saps me dry, squeezing every last drop out of me.

Panting, I flap gently this time, lowering us back to the mountainside ledge. When I land, my cock slips out of her, and Sammy gasps as my spend drips down her thighs.

"Wow," she says, admiring it. "You came a lot that time." A wicked smile crosses her face. "I have a good feeling about this."

Though I return her smile, a seed of fear sprouts in my belly. If we do succeed, I will have no more excuses to breed Sammy again.

This will all be over.

She wobbles on her feet, and I hold her up. She giggles a little drunkenly. "Wow. I've never been fucked like that in my life," she says, putting her weight on me. "Especially not in the sky. It was beautiful up there, even if I wasn't really paying attention."

I have to laugh because truthfully, neither was I. My mind was consumed by her and only her—the heave of her perfect breasts under the moonlight, how it highlighted her round cheeks and button nose, her kind spirit reaching out toward me and wrapping me up in it.

"Is there a way I could clean up?" she asks.

"Oh, of course." We didn't visit the pools earlier because there was really no need, but now I'm thrilled to show them to her. "Follow me."

SAMMY

Zakarion leads me down into the mountain, and I'm dripping his come all along the way, which makes me laugh again. My dragon smiles down at me, unabashedly revealing all of his fangs, and I just want to kiss him.

It's unfair how perfect he is. His body reads mine easily, knowing exactly what I want and how I want it. He's beautiful and majestic, and I was mesmerized by the way his black horns glimmered in the moonlight. He was fearsome, too, breathing fire into the sky when he came inside me. And I've enjoyed every moment of touring his mountain, of getting to know him even better and what makes him so unique.

Fuck. These are not good feelings. The smile falls from my mouth as we descend deeper into the cave system.

"Zak?" I ask again as we walk. "Can I stay here for the night?" I know that we have boundaries in place, but I also don't want to fly home tonight. After this, it all ends, and I want to treasure our last time together as much as possible.

He furrows his brow. "Of course. I did not expect you would want to fly home in the dark."

I nod gratefully, and find myself winding one arm around his as the torches grow fewer and farther between, so I don't get lost in the darkness.

Then, a green glow emanates from up ahead. I jog onward to find a pool of glimmering water, where I'm greeted by the smell of sulfur.

"Hot springs," Zakarion says, walking up behind me.

"They must be special hot springs to glow like that."

He laughs. "Those are stick-on lights I got at the hardware store."

Together we wade in, and it's just the perfect temperature. I find I'm a little raw between the legs as I descend deeper into the pool, and I hiss as the hot water covers me. Zakarion raises an eyebrow as he also slips one long, scaly foot into the depths.

"I'm just sore," I explain, then lower myself under the surface. He fucked me good up there, probably with more intensity than he ever has before.

My eyes roll back into my head as the water envelopes me, and I lie back against the stone to rest. Zakarion displaces a good amount of water as he takes his seat next to me.

We luxuriate in the water for a long time, simply enjoying each other's company. It's comfortable and peaceful here, not a single sound. This is the sort of isolation I craved when I bought my house out in the country—not another person for a hundred miles.

"Sammy." A quiet voice pierces the darkness. I've fallen asleep, and Zak is gently running his claws down my shoulder to wake me. "It's time for bed."

"Oh, good," I say, dragging myself out of the hot water. It's too hot now, and I'm relieved by the cool air in the cave.

"Do you want me to carry you?" my dragon asks as he supports my weight. I nod gratefully. I couldn't stand up if I tried.

"Please, I would love that."

The left side of his mouth curves up as he swoops down and swings me up into his arms, easily carrying me back the way we came. It's a long trek to his quarters, and I'm trying not to fall asleep again as he ducks through the curtain that previously cordoned off his sleeping room.

Zakarion sets me down in the nest of fur and pillows,

then spreads out and wraps his long body around me. I'm cold again since I'm still naked, and gratefully I curl up against him, soaking in the warmth of his chest.

Here, wrapped up in my dragon, it's easy to tumble away into a dream.

ZAKARION

Sammy rests so perfectly in my arms and in my bed, her shape once more conformed to mine, that it's absolutely intoxicating.

I lie awake for much too long, stroking her hair and watching her chest rise and fall, imagining what it would be like if she slept here every night. What if she were here with me in my nest while she was carrying my hatchling?

That might just be the best life possible, even if it couldn't last. Even if it ended after another fifty years, I would treasure every moment of it.

When Sammy starts to gently snore, I wind my neck around her head so my cheek lies alongside hers. Then, boldly, I wrap one arm around her, and she burrows even deeper into my embrace.

I know that we succeeded tonight. Everything felt... well, the way it should. It was right, and I was strong and virile. Like she said, I soaked her in my seed. Now she's filled with it, and surely my hatchling will start growing inside her soon. Just as powerfully as I'm certain we've created new life, I also know that this is where I'm meant to be—curled up with Sammy as we both dream.

Now how can I possibly convince her of the same?

This thought haunts me long into the night. I know she does not want the same thing I do. But I also don't know if I can live without her now.

thirteen

SAMMY

I know exactly where I am when I wake up. It's warm, so warm, and I'm pressed tight against the cream-colored scales of Zak's belly. His arms are wrapped around me, the tips of his claws resting gently on the surface of my skin. My knees are bent so that I'm straddling one of his haunches, as if he's fully ensconced me. His long neck is curved around my head so I can see his face in my peripheral vision.

That's how I notice the moment his eyes open. Those strange, lovely eyes, huge and yellow with those reptilian pupils... how have they become so seductive to me?

His eyelids lower when he sees me, and a gentle smile crosses his big snout. He squeezes me ever-so-slightly, and his long tail wraps around my thigh.

"Good morning, Sammy," Zak says, voice barely above a whisper. I just want to kiss him all over, to hold him close to me, to stay wrapped up in him forever. I want to wake up like this every morning, his gentle fire burning close by, his arms and legs curled around me.

But we have an agreement, and this is already much too intimate. I'm getting attached—so very attached to him, and it will only make our separation more painful when this is all over.

I think of his parents, how they lived and loved and then died, and I pull away. Zakarion furrows his brow and raises his head as I clear my throat and start looking around for my clothes.

"They're up in the main hall," he says, as if he can read my mind. But he still looks concerned. "Are you all right, Sammy?"

"I'm fine!" I say, too brightly, too cheerily. I don't want to bring down the good mood by telling him we've gotten too close, that I'm falling for him hard and I need to get out of here before I burrow back into that nest with him and tell him every last truth I feel.

That he's mine. That I'm his. That I don't want to live without him.

Professionalism.

"I'm going to get my clothes, then," I say, getting up to my feet. But before I can shuffle away, Zakarion wraps one big, clawed hand around my arm.

"Wait. Please."

The *please* stops me in my tracks. I glance over my shoulder, worried by the solemn tone of his voice and the frown on his face.

"What is it?" I ask, keeping my wide smile on.

"Do you..." He swallows, his long throat undulating. "Do you care for me, Sammy?"

I'm completely taken aback by his question. Of course I care about him. This one dragon's happiness means the world to me. That's the only reason I've done this, after all. I care about him and about his species.

"What do you mean?" I ask, feeling affronted. "Why else would I be here?"

Zak flinches. "That is a different kind of caring," he says, his grip loosening. "Me, as Zakarion. How do you feel about *me*?"

Oh. I think I understand what he's asking now. And I don't have a good answer.

Regardless of how I feel, I *can't* care about him that way—the way he's asking. The kindest thing I can do for him is to give him a long and fruitful life with his future child. I have to stick to the plan.

"You are a wonderful friend," I begin. That's what he is: the best friend I've ever had. I've gotten closer to him in these last few months than I ever have with anyone, and I hope that when the hatchling is born, we can stay in touch.

I see the moment the words strike him like a blunt weapon. Zakarion's eyes squeeze closed, and his hand falls away. I try to backpedal, reaching out to him, but he flinches backwards.

"I really do care about you," I say, hating the look on his face. "I enjoy all of our time together, Zak. But we made rules about this, and we can't—"

"Stop calling me that," he says suddenly, turning his head away, eyes still clamped shut.

I fall still. "Stop calling you... what?"

"That nickname." He fixes his gaze on me again, and it frightens me. I'm *afraid* of how hard and steely those reptilian eyes have suddenly become. "I don't like it."

"Zak?" I ask, and his shoulders rise up stiffly around his neck. "Oh. I'm sorry. I..." I blink back the hurt. He doesn't like it? Why didn't he tell me before? "I won't call you that again."

"Thank you," he says, but his voice is rough. He goes past

me, out through the curtain that keeps his bedroom walled off, and doesn't look back. "I'll fly you home now."

It's not a question. I watch Zakarion stalk away, and then I follow him, biting my lip so I don't cry. I'm just trying to do what's right for both of us, but I know I've hurt him.

We fly in silence, me sitting atop his back with my arms wrapped around myself because I'm freezing. I don't lean forward and cuddle into him like I did on the way here. No, I keep a polite distance between us, because Zak—no, *Zakarion*—has made it clear that "polite" is where we stand now.

I try to make friendly conversation for a few minutes, but when he gives me monosyllabic answers, I give up. We fly for some time in silence, and I let a few of my stopped-up tears flow. I've never seen Zakarion so... cold. It's like a wall of ice between us.

But I'm annoyed at him, too. What did he expect? We had an agreement when we began all of this, to protect us from this very thing.

Ahead, the wilderness gives way to civilization, and I know that I'm almost home.

Zakarion easily finds his way to my house and lands in my front yard. I slide off his back without any help or fanfare. When I peer up at him, his face is expressionless and impossible to read.

"I'll call you," I say meekly. "When I take a test next week."

He gives a sharp nod. "That would be ideal."

That's it. That's all.

"I had better go before these clouds move in," he says, glancing up at the sky, though I have a very hard time believing that a light snow would affect a dragon's flight.

"Oh," I say stupidly. "Okay."

He lets out a deep sigh, and when he looks down at me, his eyes are infinitely sad.

"Thank you for doing this for dragons like me," he says. "Be well."

And with that, he flaps his huge wings, and the gust almost knocks me over. He rises up into the sky, then zooms away—leaving me with nothing but an emptiness in my chest.

ZAKARION

I decide to stay close by to wait for Sammy's phone call. Most likely I'll have to sell off this house soon, but I will keep it until my hatchling is born so I can be near her while she carries it.

That will be torture, but she has made it clear that "close by" is all she wants from me. That was what we both agreed on. When I land, though, I am irrationally angry. Rarely in my life have I felt true *anger*, but right now I can't escape how monumentally unjust it is.

Why would Sammy have been placed in front of me that day, on that bench at DreamTogether, if this is how it was supposed to turn out?

Friend. That is how she sees me: as her friend. Despite everything we've done, all the ways we've connected, how

I've felt her heart beating so close to mine, I am not an option for her romantically.

This shouldn't come as a surprise. She's human. We have very little in common. Surely once she's finished with her obligation to me, she will move on with her life, find a human companion, and perhaps have a family of her own. One day, she will have a child who sits on that swing set out front of her house.

At the idea of someone else in Sammy's life, the flames have built up so fierce in my chest that I have to let them out or risk hurting myself. I blow a hole straight through my wall, and someone outside shrieks as my fire shoots out into the sky.

Fuck. I can't afford to get that fixed.

I wish I'd never met Sammy, so I didn't have to know what it was like to love her and not get to keep her.

I sleep and sleep, the way dragons do to pass the time. I plan on continuing this way, until my hatchling is born, and then my life will be consumed by raising my new offspring. Then I can devote all my waking hours to caring for it.

When my phone rings, I already know what Sammy is going to tell me.

"Zak!" she cries. "I mean, I'm sorry, Zakarion! Guess what, guess what?"

"What?" I ask, although I'm quite sure of the answer I'm going to get. We've managed to conceive.

"It's positive!" she crows. "You're going to have a baby!"

I should feel absolutely elated. This is what I was after, since all of this began. This is why I went to DreamTogether, why I met Sammy, and why I'm here now—for my someday-hatchling, who would complete a life that felt half-empty.

Instead, my chest is hollow, and all my emotions feel dulled. I nod my head as if Sammy can see me. *You're going to have a baby.*

Me, not *us*.

"That's wonderful news," I say, hoping I sound more excited than I feel. "I am... so glad to hear it."

There's a long silence on the other end, and I check the phone to make sure the call hasn't dropped.

"Sammy?" I ask, concerned.

"I'm here," she answers, her voice quiet. "I thought you would be happier."

Oh, hell. I cringe at how flat I sound. "I am ecstatic," I say, trying to put as much feeling into my words as I can, but even I know it doesn't sound real. "Truly."

"Okay." She sighs. "Well, I'm happy it worked. Should I give you monthly updates?"

Monthly? I would only hear from her once every month?

It feels like the bottom has fallen out of my stomach. But what did I expect? Our business together, in that way, is concluded now.

"S-sure," I answer. "Though we're no longer going through DreamTogether, you should still be receiving regular health check-ups. I can attend those with you." And I'll need some way to pay for them. She can't take that on, too.

"Okay, sounds good!" Her too-enthusiastic voice is back, the one she uses to hide her real self. "I'll make an appointment and get these results confirmed."

"Thank you, Sammy," I say, meaning it with all my heart. She is doing something selfless and marvelous for me. "Thank you so much."

"You're welcome, of course," she says in her peppy tone. "I'm glad I could help. I'll talk to you soon!"

The phone immediately goes dead. I stare down at it, and suddenly, the glass screen cracks. I drop it, realizing that I was squeezing it so hard that I broke it.

Wonderful. Now I have to get a new one so I can keep getting Sammy's calls. I'll definitely have to sell the house, with the hole in the roof and all, so I can pay for her doctor's appointments. That will mean a lot of commuting from my mountain, but I find that preferable.

At least at home it's easier to sulk. It's quiet and lonely, a perfect reflection of how I feel inside.

fourteen

SAMMY

I'D NEVER HAVE DONE IT IF I KNEW ZAKARION WOULD... WELL, not *care*.

When I called him, he sounded like I was delivering the weather report. I wonder what's changed. Before, having a hatchling of his own was all he wanted. That's why he did this, why he found me in the first place, why he went to DreamTogether at all.

I wonder if I've made a big mistake committing the next who-knows-how-many months of my life to gestating a dragon's baby, when he doesn't seem to give a shit.

When we get off the phone, I set it down neatly on the bed before finally allowing the tears rush in. I let them fall for a while, until I get tired of myself being a sad sack and make a phone call to a local ob-gyn. It's a week from now, and even though I know Zakarion said he prefers calls, I send him a text anyway. I don't know if I can bear to hear his voice right now.

> Appointment at 10am next Tuesday.

I don't get an answer. Hours later, when I still have heard no reply, I crawl under my blankets and hide there, almost wishing I'd never applied for DreamTogether, so I would never have met him.

A day later, I do get an answer:

> All right.

I grind my teeth together, my sadness and regret morphing into frustration. I shouldn't let this bother me; this was a business transaction from the very start. But the way he's treating me like a stranger hurts.

This is all for the best, then. I didn't want to fall in love with a dragon, and now any feelings I might have had for him have, thankfully, dried up. We are not even friends.

I bury myself in work, even though this early in the pregnancy, I feel like trash all the time. I can tell my body is flooding with strange hormones, making me touchy and snappish at the partygoers who get into my car. I don't get morning sickness, like I'd expected, which is my one saving grace. I do start to crave foods I don't normally eat, like barely-cooked steak, or a turkey leg right off the grill.

But as hard as I'm working, I still can't save up enough to get rid of this roofing bill and make my mortgage payment. The roofer is growing irritated with me now that the work is done. On my day off, I fix some grout in my bathroom and grease the swings on the playground so they don't squeak whenever a wind blows past.

While I sit on one, aimlessly swinging back and forth, I wonder if Zakarion will let me see the baby after its born. I run a hand over my stomach, imagining where it will grow, and at least that brings me warmth. I never imagined myself having a child before, but here I am. This one will be quite special, too, and I'm grateful I can be a part of that.

That's what I tell myself, anyway.

My friends invite me out for drinks, so I tell them about the positive test result, and they demand they come over to celebrate instead. They all bring food and bubbly water, and even homemade lemonade. I put on my best smile and pretend everything is as it should be, and this is what I wanted.

"But you've been working so much lately," Sarah says as our friends dive into a card game. "Is it really a good idea to sustain that while you're pregnant?"

"Why not?" I ask. "It doesn't change anything. My body still works fine. I'm just going to be carting around some extra weight for a while."

"I think it's a little more involved than that," she says, her brow furrowed. But I just wave her off with a smile.

That smile stays on my face as Tuesday rolls around and I head to the ob-gyn's office. It's in a monster area in the hope that the room will be big enough for Zakarion to fit, and the doctor will know what to do with a human-dragon hybrid.

When I walk into the waiting room, I find a big, red, hulking dragon sitting on the far end, in the area meant for children to play games. Even here, he's a little too big to fit. There's a very pregnant orc woman sitting there, as well as a pair of gargoyles with a toddler scrambling from one lap to another.

Zakarion's head rises when I walk in, and for a second I catch a glimpse of the old Zak. He's hopeful and excited, and I'm relieved when I see that part of him.

But then, when I sit down beside him, the smile fades and he goes as cold as a stone again.

"Sammy," he says, tipping his head. "I hope you're well?"

"Yes, yes. Doing great. Taking my vitamins and exercising." I smile and flex. "Staying strong."

He nods. "Good."

"How are you?" I venture, sitting in a nearby chair. Neither of us moves to be closer to each other.

"I am fine." He bows his head. "Thank you for doing this."

"For doing what?"

He opens his mouth, then closes it again, like he's not sure what he should say.

"It's fine," I say quickly. "I understand. You don't have to say thank you. I chose to do this, remember?"

He studies me. "Yes, you did. And I appreciate that more than you know."

Sure doesn't seem like it, I think. But I have to remember I didn't just do this just for him. Right?

We wait in silence until we're called in. The doctor is a rather tall yeti with so much hair I can barely see his eyes. He has me pee in a cup, and sends the sample away to be analyzed. Then he asks me to me lie down on the table, and brings out an ultrasound wand.

Great.

Zakarion pushes the chair next to the patient table out of

the way and sits on the floor while the doctor works, finding the right image. The yeti points at the screen.

"See, there?" he says, and we both peer at it. I don't see anything. "That's the sac where the fetus will grow. It's attached properly to the uterine lining." He smiles at both of us. "It's still very early, but all looks good. I'd like to see you again in a few weeks."

"All right," I say breezily. "Sounds good."

The doctor leaves, and I hastily put my clothes back on while Zakarion sits in the corner of the room. He doesn't speak until I've zipped up my jeans and I'm headed to the door, so I turn around and offer my most radiant smile.

"Amazing, isn't it?" I say. "We made a baby, the two of us. I didn't think it would work, and then—"

"And then you figured it out," he finishes for me. "You solved the mystery."

"We solved it together." I drop my hand to the doorknob and start to open it. "Funny thing. But I'm glad we did. See you in a few weeks?"

I try to remain cheery even though I'm dreading it. Seeing him again, all my affection—and all my squashed, hurt feelings—have risen back up to the surface. Even in this cramped room, my dragon looks majestic and beautiful.

"See you in a few weeks," Zakarion says with a resigned sigh.

I pull the door open and step out, leaving him there.

ZAKARION

The realtor insists that I have the ceiling fixed before she'll try to sell my house, but I'm tired of dealing with bureaucracy, so instead I offer a steep discount on the final sale price to anyone willing to take the house off my hands, hole and all. She doesn't like this much, but it sells quickly, and I walk away with enough cash to pay for all the medical bills that will come with Sammy's pregnancy and birth.

Once the hatchling is in my care, I'll be able to feed it and attend to its needs without piddly things like money. I will keep my hoard, and my history, and teach all of it to my hatchling. When I am finished here, there will be no reason to ever again come back to this city.

So, I return to my mountain. The first night, I don't even bother retreating down to the living quarters to sleep. I crawl on top of my hoard and lie there, hoping that when the hatchling is born and given to me, I'll finally feel the happiness I'm craving.

That's all this is: misplaced feelings. I've desired family ever since my parents died, and Sammy is the first close, intimate contact I've had since. Of course I care for her. Of course I want to hold her close, and kiss her soft, tiny mouth, and watch her get round with my hatchling in my own bed. That's natural when you haven't had enough love in your life, isn't it? You latch onto the person closest to you, and hook in because you're desperate.

We had amazing intercourse, and that's all. My affection for Sammy is simply triggered by how wonderfully she fits around my cocks. It's not about her, or her love of the countryside, or her bouncing dark curls, or her cute little house she fixed up herself, or her boundless optimism, or her generous heart—

I groan, then I close my eyes and try to crawl my way into sleep, though all I can hear are the sounds of Sammy's moans.

The week drags by slowly. I barely eat because my stomach is tied up in knots. Even my fire is quiet, my chest barely simmering. If I didn't have the regular check-ups scheduled with Sammy, I would simply go into long sleep, the hibernation that's allowed generations of dragons to pass the time quietly.

I wish I could be there, at her side, instead of moping around my mountain. I wish I could see each stage with her, curl up around her whenever she encounters difficulty. Is she sleeping? Is she eating? I hate not knowing, but I'm also too afraid to call her and find out. Just hearing her voice would make me painfully heartsick, thinking about everything I'm missing.

When our appointment rolls around, I fly back to the city slowly and lazily, because I'm both thrilled to see Sammy and frightened of it. I fear how helpless and heartsick I feel around her.

She greets me the same way as before, all smiles, without going out of her way to touch me. I don't have the energy to fake it, though, so I'm sure I have a dour expression on my face as we go into the doctor's office for her exam. She tries to keep on that smile, but even her endless cheer fades as the fetus is located, and I don't react much to seeing that it's grown larger.

Our hatchling, that we made together. I sowed it in her

under the stars that night, and at least I will always remember that.

It repeats like this, on what feels like an endless cycle. I return to my mountain and sleep, then fly to the city at the next appointment. All we're doing is walking closer to the day that Sammy and I never see each other again.

By the third visit, Sammy stops trying to be her bubbly self. We both sit in silence in the waiting room, then watch on the screen as the doctor excitedly points out our hatchling, growing inside.

"We won't know the sex until it's born, given how the genitals develop," he explains to us. "It'll be a fun surprise."

I don't like how tired Sammy appears, with dark lines under her eyes. When the doctor leaves us to let her dress again, I tap my claws together to draw her attention.

"Are you... taking care of yourself?" I ask, and I've spoken so little the last two months that my voice sounds scratchy, even to me.

She gives me a confused look. "I'm fine. I'm eating right and taking the vitamins."

My jaw flexes at the awkwardness between us. "How much are you working?" I ask.

Her brows lower. "Why?" She may be human, but I can see her hackles rising. "I have bills to pay, Zakarion."

The way she says my full name makes me ache.

"Bills?" I ask. "What sort of bills?"

"You know. Life. Had to fix my roof." She tries to shrug like it doesn't affect her, but it makes me increasingly concerned as she puts on her clothes and heads to the door. Still, I say nothing as she walks out and closes it behind her.

I was miserable for many, many years after the illness took my father. But somehow, this loneliness is worse.

Friends. We are not even that any longer.

When I return to my mountain, I stand over my hoard, surveying it. Then I pull a notebook out of my backpack, click a pen, and start writing down everything I can think of —every last piece of history, every last memory attached to each of the items in my collection.

Then I fly a little bit south, to where my phone reception is reliable, and make a call.

At the next appointment, Sammy is visibly showing. She gives me a weak greeting in the waiting room, and my heart feels sore. I return it, and once again, we pass another visit without even making eye contact.

As we head out the door and into the gently-falling snow, Sammy turns to me and waves. "Well, see you next time," she says, biting her lip before heading off toward her car.

"Wait."

She pauses. "What is it?"

I reach into my backpack and search around until my hand lands on the envelope. I withdraw it, then hold it out to her.

"Zakarion?" she asks, examining the envelope but not taking it.

"For your roof," I say. "I called those people, like you suggested. And I've started cataloguing everything in my hoard to see what belongs where. Anything that isn't significant... I've found legitimate buyers."

Her eyes widen. "You're selling off your treasure?" She looks at the envelope with even more confusion. "Why?"

I thrust the money into her hand, and she squeaks as I trap it there. "Take it," I tell her firmly. "Please."

Her brows crease as I release her, and she takes the envelope gently. Her lashes are wet and her eyes are red when she looks up at me again.

"Okay," she finally says. "Thank you."

Then she turns and walks away into the snow.

I have to hope this will all get better when my hatchling is with me. Then I'll have a purpose and a reason to live. I watch her get into her car, wishing I could go with her, that I could curl around her as the weather gets colder and keep both of my woman and my hatchling warm.

Eventually, I flap my wings and take off into the sky, letting the snow wash over me.

fifteen

SAMMY

IT IS MORE THAN ENOUGH MONEY TO PAY OFF THE ROOFER, including the interest he's now decided I owe him. I don't even know what to do with the rest of it. I pay down my mortgage, then save the rest for groceries and bills.

At least now I don't have to work so much, but that leaves far more time for sitting around feeling sorry for myself.

"All right, that's it." Sarah stands up straight in her lawn chair, surprising all of us. I bought take-out, hoping some friend time might be what I need after my last visit to the ob-gyn. "I'm tired of you moping around all the time."

It's the dead of winter now, but I insist on continuing to get plenty of sunlight and vitamin D. Sometimes that means bundling up, clearing away the snow, and lying in lawn chairs in my yard.

"Moping?" I ask, sitting up. "I'm not moping."

"You've been moping for *months*." She fastens a hard glare on me. "I wish you'd never agreed to do this. Carrying that dragon's baby has been nothing but misery for you since day one."

I frown. "I'm fine. Really. My feet aren't bothering me, I haven't even had morning sickness, and—"

"Not that kind," Sarah says, letting out a defeated sigh. "Why don't you see him anymore?"

I frown at her. Jared finally returns from getting himself a new hot cocoa. He refuses to sit out here with us, but he likes to be a part of the gossip.

"Because of fe-e-e-elings," Jared sing-songs. "You know, for such a lovable person, you really don't hand out your love easily, Sam."

"Stop ganging up on me," I grumble.

"It's true, though," Sarah says, rubbing her chin. "I think he's onto something. You've been avoiding Zakarion ever since you got pregnant. Why? Clearly you had a thing for him."

"That's the problem!" I could just scream. "I can't have a *thing* for a dragon who's three hundred years old, and will live until he's a thousand years old. That's a whole ass *millennium*! I'm like a blip on the radar for him."

Jared and Sarah both stare at me with wide, confused eyes.

"Huh?" Jared says, breaking the silence. "That's what you're worried about?"

I don't understand why they don't get it. "Of course it is! I want to find my forever person, you know? I don't want to commit to someone when I'm just going to die on them." I don't even mention the other part—that if Zakarion were to bond to me, it could spell his end, too.

With a heavy sigh, Sarah drags her lawn chair closer to mine and wraps an arm around my shoulders, pulling me tight against her.

"Sammy. You fucking idiot." She pats my head. "I say that as affectionately as possible. You can't keep pretending you don't like him, putting on that fake-happy face while you burn up inside. Remember what happened last time?"

Ugh. I know she's right. At the gym, I faked it and faked it until I couldn't take it anymore, and I burst apart at the seams. The last thing I want is to explode on Zakarion.

"Have you told him this fear of yours?" Sarah asks.

"It's not a fear, it's a fact!" I snap.

"Stop for a second." She tightens her grip in a rather threatening manner. "Have you told him, or not?"

I cross my arms petulantly. "Why would I? It doesn't matter. It would never work. It's not worth it to even open the door."

Jared pipes up. "But what if you opened the door and found something wonderful on the other side?"

But I don't see anything wonderful. All I see is heartbreak, and I don't want to do that to him, or to me.

I decide to pick up snowshoeing, despite my growing belly. It's only five more months now, according to the ob-gyn—just five more months until I have the baby, and never see Zakarion again.

I lose myself in the woods, following trails that others have left to tiny lodges where I can build a fire and warm up. Nature is mostly silent save for the occasional bird call, which reminds me there's still life out there, even in the dead of winter.

Often, though, when it's cold, I think of how warm

Zakarion is, how the fire in his chest would keep me toasty even as the snow falls.

While our next appointment rolls around, and the little dragon inside me grows bigger, I debate this question. What would Zakarion do if I told him? Would if he returned my feelings? Then what?

I'm terrified of the idea of telling him the truth—and even more terrified of him saying, *but you're human*. He'd be right. I'm nothing, a drop in the bucket of time. He has ancient treasures in his house that date back thousands of years, while I'll be lucky if I get another sixty or seventy out of my life here on earth.

But Sarah's right. I can't keep doing this any longer.

Finally, it's Tuesday. I drive to the doctor's office with a hard lump in my throat, dreading what I'm going to say. When Zakarion arrives and enters the lobby, all I want to do is throw my arms around his neck and hug him for everything he's worth.

I offer him a smile, same as always. "How are you?"

"I'm well," he says, his mouth in that same hard line that I've grown accustomed to, his eyes giving nothing away. "And you?"

"I'm good. Trying to stay warm. At least the snowpack has been good for outdoors sports."

He frowns deeper. "You have been out doing sports?" His eyes travel down to my belly. "Is that wise?"

I swat at him playfully. "I'm pregnant, not a porcelain doll. It's good for me to get exercise."

He furrows his brow. "But nothing strenuous, right?"

"Right," I say, letting out a small laugh. "Don't worry, Zak." I want to slap myself. "Zakarion. Sorry."

His eyes close and he sighs, as if he's very tired and my

calling him that didn't help. I ball my hands up in my lap, wondering how things became this way between us. I feel like I don't know him anymore.

Neither of us speaks until we're called back into the doctor's office. Once I'm in a gown, the yeti returns to do the ultrasound. Zakarion sits in his usual place next to me as the ob-gyn covers my belly in gel and starts scanning it.

"Oh, wow." I can't help the exclamation as the baby appears on-screen. It's much bigger than before, with definite features—wings, a tail, even a snout. I gape at what I'm seeing, this little fetus curled up in a ball inside me.

"Cool, huh?" the yeti says, pulling the instrument away. The screen goes dark. He presses some buttons, and a photo he took pops back up. I reach out to touch the screen, where the little baby dragon's head is curled down so its body forms an egg shape. "I'll leave you two alone for a few minutes before we talk next steps?"

I nod, and the doctor departs. When he's gone, I study the picture further, then turn to Zakarion. His eyes aren't fixed on the screen, but on his hands where they're clasped tightly together.

Why isn't he happy? Why isn't he enjoying this, seeing our kid for the first time? I wish I understood.

I slide my hand into his, and his head jerks up in surprise. I pull away his thumb, as it's the most I can get my fingers around, and drag it towards my belly. There I place his hand flat, and his big, yellow eyes widen.

"Sammy?" he asks, uncertainty in his voice.

I put my palm on his knuckles and try to smile, but there's too much sadness behind it to hold it for long.

"Neat, isn't it?" I ask, trying not to sound as nervous as I feel. "We made this."

He nods in agreement, but his face shows very little. I sigh, and my shoulders sag. This is supposed to be happy, that we succeeded, that dragons will continue on for another generation.

I need to say it, or I might just burst.

"Zakarion?"

He tries to pull his hand away, but I don't let him.

"What is it?" he asks, clearly perplexed by this extended contact.

"I lied to you." What an opener.

Zakarion frowns even further. "You lied? When?"

"When you asked how I felt." I take a mighty breath, trying to shore up my strength for what I have to say. "And I said you were my friend."

His hand jerks under mine like he's about to pull it back, but I press down, keeping him anchored to my belly. His wide eyes find mine again.

"I didn't mean it," I say, and I can't stop the tears now squeezing out and tumbling down my cheeks. Zakarion inhales sharply. "That wasn't true at all. You're so much more than a friend to me. So, so much more. And—"

A sob I didn't expect cuts me off. Now he looks more worried than surprised, and his other hand reaches out to land on my shoulder.

"Sammy...?" he asks, tilting his head to one side, confusion twisting his face.

"And..." I hiccup, trying to get the words out. "And... I think... I think that I probably..."

I'm too busy crying now to finish my sentence. Suddenly arms wrap around me, and Zakarion pulls me roughly against his body, though I'm still halfway on the doctor's table. His claws sink into my shirt, and his long neck curls down to fully embrace me. "Sammy," he says, his voice miserable. "Don't cry. Please don't cry."

"I c-can't help i-it." I hiccup again, now in the middle of a full-blown episode. Fucking hormones. "I h-hate not... not talking to you. I hate h-how cold it is between us. I miss you. I miss you so much, Zak." I slap my hand over my mouth. "I'm sorry, I keep forgetting—"

"It's fine. Shh." He wraps his arms even tighter around me, and the warmth of his chest feels so, so good against my cheek. "You can call me whatever you want, Sammy. I'm the one who's sorry."

"For what?" I sniff, wiping away my tears.

"For making you cry." He leans back, and raises his head to get a good look at me. "I didn't know you were holding all this inside."

"You don't hate me?" I ask, perplexed.

He looks equally as taken aback. "Hate you...?" Sadness fills his eyes. "You thought I hated you?"

"I don't know!" I sniffle again as I try to right myself on the patient table. "Either me, or the hatchling, or both of us."

His mouth falls open. "No!" He fervently shakes his head. "Oh, no. That's the opposite of the truth."

I wipe my snot away with my sleeve. "Then what is the truth?"

Zakarion closes his eyes, and his shoulders drop like he's given up on something he's been holding onto tightly. "I care about you far too much," he says, so quietly I have to strain to hear him. "Far, far too much."

"Too much?" I ask. Then why has he behaved this way, like we're strangers?

"I want you." He drops his head low, refusing to hold my gaze. "I want you more than I've ever wanted anyone. But you made it clear that's not what you need."

Oh.

I throw my arms around his neck for real this time, and sink against him. He tentatively puts his arms around me in return, holding me close to his chest.

"I think," I say finally, swallowing hard, "I think that I love you, Zak."

sixteen

ZAKARION

SHE LOVES ME.

My heart soars. It sings. It does loop de loops in the air with wild joy knowing that Sammy loves me as I love her.

I kiss her hair, burying my face in it, squeezing her tight against me. I could simply absorb her into my body to keep her and our hatchling close to me forever. She squeaks as I envelop her completely, dragging her off the doctor's table and firmly into my lap.

"Sammy," I murmur, stroking her back and her head and every part of her I can reach. "I think I've loved you since the day I saw your face."

She pulls away enough that she can look up at me, and though her eyes are red and brimming with tears, there's a broad smile on her perfect, round cheeks.

"But you didn't even know me!"

I shake my head. "All I had to see was that hope and joy in your eyes and I knew." I was a goner from the beginning.

Her smile wavers, though.

"But what does that mean... in the long term?" she asks, uncertain. "You may love me now, but what about when I get old, and you don't?"

I don't understand the question. "Why would it change?" I ask. When dragons find their heart bond, very little can tear it apart. "I love you for *you*, Sammy. Even when you're wrinkled and gray." I like the idea of that, actually—the two of us getting older, surrounded by our hatchlings. If she truly feels what she says she does, I plan to plant many more of them in her.

"But then... what happens when..." She sniffles again as a fresh wave of tears stream down her face. "When I die? I don't want to take you with me. I couldn't do that."

My heart breaks looking into her sweet, dark eyes. I understand so much more now. Is this why she kept me at arm's length? Because she feared our future?

"When you die, you will be surrounded by those that love you," I tell her. I hold her cheeks in my big hands, and brush my snout over the tip of her nose. "My heart will always be filled with you, for all of my days."

Her gaze softens. "How are you so certain of that?"

"It's been clear to me for a long time now." I cradle her belly between us, tracing the shape of it with my index claw. "This hatchling was made from love. I know that in my soul." I pick up her hand and press it to my chest, where my fire simmers. "And as long as it breathes, there will always be a part of us that lives on, no matter what becomes of us."

Tears are dribbling down her face, trailing over her plump lips as she smiles back at me.

"That's a nice way to think of it," she says, raising one hand to run it down the side of my snout. I lean into her, and the feel of her soft skin against my scales makes my body think other, dirtier things.

Gently I lift her off my lap and place her back on the patient table so my cocks don't get any funny ideas, which is as good a moment as any for the ob-gyn to return. He brushes some of his long, white hair away from his eyes, and takes in the sight of Sammy's small hand clasped in mine with a wry grin.

"Would you like me to print this for you so you can take it home?" he asks, gesturing at the picture on the screen.

Sammy's face lights up. "I would love that!"

I take in the sight of our hatchling again, curled up small in her belly, and squeeze her hand. Soon, everything will be how it should be.

SAMMY

I hang the print up on my refrigerator using some quirky tourist magnets Sarah got for me when she took a road trip to Connecticut. I simply stare at it, tracing the lines around the baby's shape.

Hot breath tickles the back of my neck, and claws click on the linoleum.

"Ours," Zak says, resting his huge head on top of mine so we can look at it together. His arms wrap around my waist, bringing me tight against his oh-so-warm body. "We did that, together. And we'll raise it together, love it together."

A shiver travels across my body, then I spin around to press myself fully against him. *My dragon.* He wants to be mine, and I want to be his.

"I'm so glad you're here," I whisper to him. I lean back so I can peer up into his face, and his nostrils are flared, steam rising up from them. Standing up on my toes, I take his long snout in my hands and press a kiss to his snout.

"Sammy," he breathes, his eyes closing. "I want to be wherever you are. I want to take care of you and the hatchling forever."

This makes me pause and think. I want to be where he is, too—but we live in quite different places.

"What about your house?" I ask. "The one in the city?"

With a miserable sigh, Zak shakes his head. "I had to sell it."

That just leaves my home, where he's certainly too tall to live... or his mountain.

I snap my fingers. "All right," I say with a new sureness in my voice. "Then I should relocate. I'll keep the house, of course, but maybe until the hatchling is born, I should stay with you?"

I adore how his smile shows off all of his gleaming fangs.

"Of course. Please. I would love that." This time, he's the one who kisses me, though his lips don't have the same dexterity that mine do—it's more like a gentle nudge on the mouth. "My home is your home. Everything that I have... it's yours."

I gape at him. "You don't mean that. You have more treasure than a king."

But Zak just shrugs. "What does any of it matter if you can't share it with someone you love?"

Just the word sends a tingle down my spine, and even further to the valley between my legs. All this mushy stuff is really turning me on. When Zakarion wraps his arms around me, I suggestively rub my butt against his groin. He responds with a grunt, and his movements mimic mine. Soon I feel two objects nudge at my backside, and fuck, all the time apart is catching up to me right now.

I don't wait to strip off my shirt. Zakarion's head jerks up at the sight of me—and he bumps his horns right into the ceiling.

"Oh, hell," he says, rubbing his head. I giggle, grab his hand, and pull him down to the carpet with me in the living room. When my pants are off, I find his cocks have fully emerged from his slit, and already there are twin droplets of pre-come dripping down the front. I lift my ass and bring my knees up to his hips, but Zak stops me.

Instead of fucking me, like I've been aching for, his black tongue flicks out from between his teeth like he's tasting the air. He pulls my legs wide apart, exposing my pussy to the whole living room, and drool pools in his fangs.

"My Sammy," he whispers, arching his long neck down between my thighs. He brushes his snout over the gentle swell of my belly, letting out a satisfied sigh from deep in his chest. "What a beautiful, wonderful thing we've made."

That tongue darts out again, and he sniffs his way lower until his tongue is snaking around my clit. When I moan, it slips inside me and ventures around until I'm twitching and writhing.

"Zak!" I cry out.

He sits up suddenly, licking his lips. "What? What is it?"

"Please, please fuck me."

His gaze turns wicked, and he sits up, my juices still dripping from his snout. Zakarion hooks his hands underneath me and pulls my hips towards him, where his cocks are both waiting for me.

"Someday," he muses, using both knobby heads to brush over my clit, again and again, "I'm going to take you with both of them."

I could jump for joy. "At the same time?" I ask hopefully.

His long neck curls down toward me, so he's looking into

my eyes. "At the same time. For now, though..." He fits the head of his lower cock into me, so the upper one lands between my legs, over my bush. "I'm going to fuck you until you're screaming my name."

And he does. Oh, he does, sliding that cock into me farther and farther, spreading me for his swell, burying himself in me up to the hilt where my pussy swallows all of him.

While he fucks me mercilessly, I draw a hand up to his cheek. He slows his pace as his yellow, reptilian eyes focus on me. I tell him everything with that look, every last drop of love I feel, and he returns it just as fiercely.

My dragon.

ZAKARION

My Sammy, her big breasts bouncing underneath me, her swollen belly jiggling with every thrust of my hips—how I love her. Looking into those bright, dark brown eyes of hers, taking in all the unguarded adoration plain on her face...

Oh, hell. I'm done.

My whole body seizes, and I'm muttering apologies as my cocks both swell up. I thrust into Sammy with wild abandon, and she cries out as I shove myself deep, and then, I burst. But I know she's close, so I grit my teeth and keep driving into her, all while smothering my sensitive upper cock against her clit. My seed is pouring out of her, squelching loudly as I fuck her as hard as I can, pushing through how over-sensitive both my cocks are. As I pound into her over and over, my claws gripping the carpet, her eyes roll back into her head. She screams out, "Zak!"

Then Sammy clamps down hard around me, her mouth wide open. She's so tight and so slick that stars pop in front of my eyes. Somehow, my whole body tightens up, and I roar as I unleash a second time, tearing the carpet out with my claws. My climax is even bigger than before, a monstrous wave that envelops both of us and drags us out to sea.

I have to hold myself up on my elbows so I don't crush her, panting as hard as I am. Sammy is gasping with her exertion, too, and eventually her big eyes open again.

She smiles shyly. "Wow. That was amazing." She slides her hand up my snout to my cheek, and I can't help nuzzling it in return.

"You are amazing," I tell her, trying my best to kiss her small lips. It feels so good just to *kiss* Sammy, and I never realized how much I craved this intimacy with her.

Eventually, I'm able to slip my cocks free, and soon they both retract into my slit once more, vanishing. Sammy grins widely.

"So cool," she murmurs, then pulls me in close to her. It's a feeble gesture with how much bigger I am, but I pretend that she's able to do it, and curl myself around her small body. I place one big hand over the hatchling growing in her belly, and know I'm right where I'm supposed to be.

SAMMY

WE WASTE NO TIME IN MOVING FORWARD. WE BOTH WANT THE same thing—to sleep together every night, to enjoy each other's company, to raise our hatchling together—and so that night, we gather up my essentials into a backpack, and fly back together toward Zakarion's mountain. I hold onto his neck tight as we fly, soaking up his warmth, and he strokes my arm with one clawed hand as he carries us over the mountain range.

When we land, though, I'm surprised to find that his hoard has shrunk dramatically.

"How much have you given away?" I ask, a little horrified to see so much of it gone.

Zakarion shrugs. "I have been making an inventory and providing it to that gryphon from the Department of Antiquities, and they tell me which items have cultural or historical significance." He wrinkles his nostrils as he picks up a small notebook. "Still don't like that guy much, though."

When he hands me the notebook, I open it to find more

than just a list. Each page contains a detailed history of some item from Zak's hoard—which of his family members acquired it, and how long it had been a part of the collection. He's written what he can about not just each item, but those who loved them. The pages detail how his mother loved art, how his grandfather had an affinity for rubies; all memories of those who have long passed.

"I realized that what was important to me was the connection it gave me to the past," Zakarion says, looking wistfully at what remains of his hoard. "Not the objects themselves. I will pass this on to my hatchling, so they can know and remember, too. Then the memories will never be lost."

I pass back the notebook, and he clutches it to his chest before placing it on a stand nearby.

"You've done a good thing," I tell him, stroking his arm. "You've changed the world and made it a better place."

He offers me a sad smile. "I hope so. Though what truly makes everything better is having you here."

I can't help but swoon. Suddenly, Zakarion hefts me into his arms, and I squeak and grab him around the neck. His chest rumbles as he chuckles.

"Where are we going?" I ask, my backpack still sitting on the floor.

"To our room," he says. "Where I've been wanting to make love to you since I met you."

A romantic, my dragon. I bury my face in his warm chest as he carries me down to the room with the curtain, and fulfills his promise of telling me with his body just how much he loves me.

Zakarion painstakingly carries most of my belongings from my house to the mountain, making multiple trips to ferry all of my most important possessions. "I want you to feel at home," he said when I objected to how much he was bringing with him. "I want you to know that all of this is yours, too."

I want to say it's the hormones that makes me tear up when he talks tells me these things, but I know it's not just that. His heart is so big and so tender, I feel as if I've been given a precious gift.

And damn, the view. I don't know if I'll ever get over it. In the mornings, Zakarion lights the fire under the kettle for me, and I make decaf coffee in the french press. Then we sit together on the ledge that overlooks the mountain range, fog rising up and dissipating as the morning sun peeks in. On mornings like that, I curl up against Zak's warm body, and he wraps an arm around me, resting his thumb across my swollen belly.

I love it out here, so far from civilization. The night sky is vast and unmarred, the air silent save for the occasional animal call. I buy groceries every week in the city, but Zakarion hunts a good bulk of our food, which is wonderful when some red, barely-cooked meat is all my body wants right now. I'm getting big and bulky these days, and the hunger grows more ever-present.

He also brought me... a present.

Most of the time we make love in the nest, down inside the mountain, and it's here that Zak pulls out an unusual purchase: a series of small butt plugs.

"Both at the same time," I murmur, taking them like a sacred object. He nods rapidly, showing all his fangs when he smiles.

"Both at the same time," he agrees.

We experiment with them, one at a time, working me up from the smallest to the largest. Zakarion loves to bury one of his cocks in me, the plug worked into my ass while he fucks me, his big hands holding my belly.

At night, when my body starts to feel sore from lugging around a basketball-sized baby, we lie in the hot spring together, me sitting in his lap. He's assured me that exposing our hatchling to high temperatures is not only good for a young dragon, but essential from time to time for healthy growth.

As we lie there together, his tail wraps around my ankle, and he lowers his head to breathe into my hair. We stay like that until I fall asleep, then Zakarion carries me back to our bed.

One night, after a relaxing hot spring session, I wake up to Zak looking down into my face. He quickly turns away, as if I've caught him sneaking a cookie.

"What is it?" I ask, patting his long snout to make sure he's all right. He huffs.

"Just... watching you." He strokes my side, down to my stomach, which has been growing faster now. Our latest ultrasounds show even more detail, from the longer neck to the curled-up wings. The doctor ensures me they won't present a problem during birth, nestled inside its thick sac. It's halfway between an egg and a placenta, he explained. I just shook my head in wonder.

"Are you watching me sleep?" I ask. "How romantic."

Zakarion snorts, then leans down to kiss my lips, his big nostrils bumping my nose. "You're so beautiful," he murmurs, tangling his claws in my hair as he slides his arm beneath my head. "That's all that's on my mind."

"Not fucking me with both cocks at the same time?" I ask jokingly. But his expression is far more serious.

"That, too." I notice that his slit has already opened, revealing the two treasures hiding inside. His tender grip on me turns into his claws dragging over my skin, leaving long lines behind. My body sags into his touch, hungry for the feel of him around me, inside me, consuming me. I could get lost in Zakarion easily, and I almost do as he runs his hand down my back, to the cleft of my ass. There, he pushes my cheeks apart.

"Are you ready for me?" he asks, running a knuckle down between them. "Do you think you can take both my cocks, little Sammy?"

I whimper at just the suggestion, my whole body still warm from the hot springs and getting warmer. "Yes," I tell him, urgently pressing my bottom against his hand. "Please, I'm ready for you."

"Get on your knees."

Oh, I love when Zak tells me what to do. Obediently I crawl onto my hands and knees, raising my hips into the air for him. He sucks in a harsh breath as he looks down at me.

"Hell," he mutters. "I've dreamed of this." He lines himself up behind me, his tail lashing back and forth with anticipation and disrupting our nest of blankets. I'm surprised when I feel the sloped-up tip of his upper cock already slipping into my pussy.

"I need to get it wet first," he says into my ear, pushing only a fraction of the way inside me, like he always does. I shudder at the suggestion as he tests my depths, inching in farther and farther with each gentle stroke. Soon I'm moaning into the pillows, pushing my hips back to try to take even more of him. He chides me.

"You'll have it when I say so." He pushes in deeper, claiming more of me, teasing me with his swell. My body is well-accustomed to his now, and it doesn't take much for it to slip through. Zak can't help a groan as he sinks all the way in, up to the narrow base of his cock.

Then, abruptly, he pulls it free, and I gasp at the sudden loss of him. I turn my head to object, only to find him fiddling with a bottle of lube to get the cap open.

It's so adorable that I giggle as I reach out and pop the lid. Gratefully he takes it back and slathers his hand in it, which he then uses to stroke himself. When all of his rounded nubs are thoroughly glistening, he drags his cock up to the small, puckered hole we've been playing with so diligently. He tests it, just pressing in the flared head. Already I feel the bite, the stretch, the feeling that something foreign is invading. Like we practiced, though, I try to breathe deep and relax, letting myself open for him.

Even the biggest one of the plugs isn't as broad as Zakarion is, and when he presses in farther, I let out a sharp cry. Immediately he reels back, but I grab his arm before he can get too far.

"It's okay," I say, panting. I close my eyes and take a few heavy breaths. "More lube. Try again."

"If you're certain," he says, but obediently picks up the bottle, dribbles more lube over both of us, and positions himself once more.

It slides in even deeper, even easier this time, and he stops at the same place he did before.

"More," I whimper, trying to slow my rapidly-beating heart. "Give me more, please!"

He groans, and pushes in further. Oh, it's so much, so much I feel like I might burst open and maybe do some lower body functions that I shouldn't, but it's also so *good*. I buck underneath him, and he accidentally slips in deeper.

"Oh, hell, Sammy," he mutters, pulling out ever-so-slowly and then thrusting back in again, to the same depth. "You feel amazing."

"You know... what would feel..." I moan as he fills me even fuller in that place that's only reserved for him. "...really good?"

He sinks in again, and I can feel the swell of him starting to work its way through. But I'm still so tight, so he doesn't push, and leans forward to rest his head on my shoulder.

"What would that be?" he asks in his bedroom voice.

"If you put... the other one in now."

Zakarion chuckles, his hot breath tickling my neck. He gently pulls his hips back, so he's nearly leaving me. Keeping the head of his upper cock inside my ass, he drags the lower one across my clit, up to my needy pussy. It's wet and hungry for him, and he obliges me by pressing gently inside.

Those two heads lodged in me just about ruins me. My whole body goes tight, and Zak groans.

"I've fantasized for so long about this," he murmurs, stroking my sides, my ass. With admirable restraint, he pushes in very slowly, asking both parts of me to open wide for him.

The volley of sheer sensation that overwhelms me nearly takes me under. I cry out as the pressure of both his thick cocks builds, and when he sinks in just an inch further...

It's too much. I clench hard around him, and my dragon moans, even though he's barely halfway sheathed in me. He pumps his hips, bursting through my orgasm, sliding in even deeper with both at the same time. Those twin swells are urging me apart, the nubs stimulating every last inch of me, turning me into what feels like a vortex of time and space.

"You feel incredible," he says as he gently rocks back and forth, nursing my orgasm and letting me come down at the same time. "I can't believe how tight you are. How well you fit my cocks. Both of them." He presses forward, going deeper, and I can feel the nubs on his lower cock rubbing against the nubs on his upper cock through me, and I think it's impossible to be more obscenely filled than I am now.

And then, he starts to thrust. Slowly at first, in and out in a slow, gentle motion that has me careening towards my finish again. I'm dizzy now, barely holding myself up, as he moves faster, and I think I can't possibly climax again or I might pass out.

"Zakarion, I love you, I love you so much," I'm moaning and crying, tears starting to stream down my face as he moves faster, and faster. "Oh, fuck, I can't, I—"

His neck curls down and he brushes the back of my head with his nose. "I love you, too, Sammy," he whispers to me. "My heart and body were both made for you. To please you. To care for you. Now come for me."

When he meets his finish, roaring like a beast and plunging both his cocks into me, I orgasm so hard that my vision temporarily goes white, and a shockwave travels from my throat all the way to my toes. I scream his name, and he groans like a pained animal, thrusting once, twice more, drawing my pleasure out in front of me like a road that never ends.

At last, I collapse, completely gelatinous. Zakarion very gently withdraws himself, and my ass is so reluctant to let him go that I whine as he pulls free. While I lie there in a puddle, he retrieves a towel and cleans us both off, then slides me across the blankets and pillows into his arms.

While we spoon, his big hand curls underneath my belly. "I can't wait to meet our hatchling." His claws drift up my breasts, and he gently lifts one. "And you'll feed it so well with these."

I giggle. "Who would have guessed?" Everything feels so

absolutely wonderful right now, like liquid starlight, and I close my eyes as I sink even deeper into Zakarion and his perfect, comforting warmth.

"Mmm," he answers, nuzzling my head. "Miraculous."

I fall asleep like that, tangled up with my dragon, curled around our baby, right where I was meant to be all along.

eighteen

ZAKARION

IT IS MARVELOUS WATCHING SAMMY GROW, HER BREASTS changing shape as her belly swells even larger. Our ultrasounds are more exciting every time as our hatchling develops, and soon my Sammy is full to bursting. She grumps sometimes about the weight of it, the awkwardness of her body, the aches and pains that accompany carrying it around with her. I do what I can, but she knows she simply has to bear it. The time is coming that it will be over, and we'll finally be united with our young.

She's kept her house, and we've paid it off through fully legal means, though she plans to live full-time at the mountain while we raise the hatchling. We still meet her friends once every few weeks, and my sheer size has finally stopped surprising them. Now we all sit in Sammy's yard together as the weather grows warmer and shoots come up out of the ground.

"You should give us a tour of the mountain sometime," Sarah says. "It sounds like the perfect place for you, Sam."

She preens. "We would love that. Maybe we need to get a road built after all, Zak?"

Of course, I'll do whatever she asks. "As you wish."

Though she's quite pregnant, Sammy loves to go explore the wilderness, and I often hike along with her as we search out placid lakes and ancient trees. Sometimes when her feet are tired, she sits on my back while I walk on four legs, and then I fly us home.

We're eating dinner one night when Sammy abruptly freezes. She winces, and then her eyes go wide.

"Zak," she whispers. "I just felt it."

I tilt my head. "Felt what?"

"The thing. The, um, contraction? I think?"

It's like a switch is flipped in my brain. There's a go bag for this exact occasion stashed in a basket in the main hallway, and I rush to grab it as Sammy gets out of her chair. We leave the food on the table as I scoop her up into my arms, the bag in her lap, and I leap off the ledge into the sky.

My great wings carry us quickly to the city as I fly faster than I've ever flown before. Every few minutes Sammy wriggles in my arms, clearly uncomfortable with her body's signals.

"We're almost there," I tell her as I swoop down. The hospital isn't far, but Sammy's little whimpers are already escalating.

"I don't know, Zak," she says in a worried voice. "Something's happening. It hurts. It hurts so much."

I curse to myself, but try to keep my face schooled in a calm expression. "Don't worry. The doctors will know what to do."

I carry her right in the front doors of the hospital, not putting her down until a gurney is wheeled out for her. After we're taken to a room, a doctor comes in—a big wolfman with a mask over his snout.

"What have we here?" he asks, immediately seating himself between Sammy's legs. He glances at me, then at the human in front of him. "Ah, a dragon hybrid?"

"Yes, it's mine," I say quickly. The wolfman smiles under his mask.

"Then this might be a bit of a challenge." He spreads Sammy's legs to take a peek, and then his eyes get huge. "Oh. Okay. We're going, are we?"

"Going? Where?" Sammy asks, concerned.

"This baby is coming out, pronto." The ob-gyn hops to his feet and calls out into the hallway for a nurse. A whole team assembles around us, and now I'm starting to wonder if this was a good idea. Is Sammy in danger?

"Zak," she moans, reaching for my hand. I encompass it in both of mine, stroking her comfortingly. "I don't want to do it." She sounds so miserable and helpless. "It hurts."

"I know." But there's nothing I can do for her except to stay at her side. "It won't last long."

"For once," the wolfman says, "you're right. This baby is exiting stage left as quickly as possible."

Then Sammy shrieks, and my heart feels like it might just break in half seeing her in so much pain. All I can do is clasp her hand in mine and hope everything will be all right in the end.

SAMMY

It is fucking misery, giving birth to a dragon's baby. I want to beat him senseless for putting this thing inside me, all while I cling to him like we're trapped in a hurricane.

There's no fucking way I'm having any more of them. Just no way. The doctor didn't even have time to give me an epidural, and I've never been so angry in my life.

I sob and cry and Zakarion wipes away my tears as my whole body tries to accommodate.

"Don't worry," he croons. "You can do this. I know it."

I'm not so sure, though.

"Should have done a fucking C-section," I mutter.

But I do survive it. With Zak at my side, I push and push, sweating and cursing, until finally...

"It's here!" I exhale with the world's deepest relief as, finally, I feel my baby emerge. The wolfman hurriedly calls over a nurse. "We have to open the egg sac."

Time passes, and I'm worried when I don't hear a sound. But Zakarion is rubbing my hand, assuring me everything is fine.

Then I hear a chirp. A nurse kneels down next to the bed, carrying a tiny, red bundle in her arms. She holds it out to me, and there are already more tears building behind my eyes as I take it from her.

"We think it's male, but it's hard to tell still," the fairy nurse says. Our infant keens again. "He needs some food now. Here, let me show you."

Zakarion watches with fascination as our toothless hatchling latches onto my nipple, and a relieved sigh falls from my lips finally feeling him in my arms. Zak leans down and rubs his nose on my cheek.

"You did it," he says fondly, stroking my hair with one hand, and caressing the baby's little body with the other.

I nod as joyous tears fall from my eyes. I can't speak, too overcome by my happiness at having both of them here with me, at last.

We get to go home the next day, but there were some... consequences to having such a large child, and I'm not in the best shape when Zakarion carries both of us back to the mountain. Our infant screeches for much of the journey before I pull up my shirt and feed him again.

"How long until he can fly on his own?" I ask.

"Five years at least."

I exhale. "That's good. I don't think I could handle a flying toddler."

When we've landed on the ledge outside our home, Zakarion doesn't set me down. It'll be a little while before I can walk properly, the wolfman cautioned me, but Zak was more than happy to agree to carrying me around until then.

At last, I'm back in our nest, with our hatchling curled up between us. As he sleeps, we debate what to call him.

"Dragonkind create new names by merging the parents' names," he explains.

"So, what? Zakamy? Samarion?" Both of them sound silly. "I'm not a dragon, though, so my name isn't great for this."

Zakarion hums as he thinks. "Zantha," he says suddenly. "Zan, for short."

I kind of like it. It's a suitable name for one of the world's remaining majestic dragons.

"All right. Zantha." I pull him closer, reveling in his baby smell. "I suppose he should go in his own nest, hmm?"

Zakarion agrees, and takes him to the smaller pile of pillows and blankets we've placed inside a big basket. I was concerned at first about this arrangement, but everything I've ever learned about human babies is out the window now. Happily, Zan curls up, tail wrapping around his tiny head with the barely-noticeable black nubs that will eventually become his horns.

Then my dragon leads me back to our bed, and wraps me up tight.

"Thank you," he says, cradling my head against his warm, thrumming chest. "Thank you for everything, Sammy."

I nuzzle into him deeper. "You don't need to thank *me*. It's not every day you find a husband with two dicks."

He chuckles, sending a rumble down his throat and into his ribcage. "Husband, hmm?"

"Yeah." I smile against him. "I don't need a ceremony, though. My folks wouldn't make the trip anyway. But I know it in my heart."

"As do I," Zakarion says. "All of me belongs to you, and our hatchlings."

"Hatchlings, plural?" I say, snorting. "It'll be a while before you can convince me that's a good idea."

He chuckles, and I fall asleep like that, curled up at my dragon's side.

nineteen

SAMMY

I WISH SOMEONE HAD TOLD ME THAT DRAGON HATCHLINGS ARE nothing like human babies. From the very first day we brought him home, Zan has been a terror who moves at the speed of light. He was born with a full range of movement, allowing him to skitter away the second I turn my attention to something else. Zak spends an inordinate amount of time looking through caves for him.

When the hatchling nurses, he grabs onto my boobs with his tiny hands, now starting to grow tiny claws, and sucks for all he's worth. I cringe as he digs in, and we start putting little mittens on him so he can't do any damage.

Soon, I've healed enough that I can bring Zakarion inside me again, and we both moan with bliss as we're reunited. Nothing will ever feel as good as one—or both—of his cocks, with their nubs and swells, pushing inside me. It's been so long that Zak goes off early, as he has the tendency to do, but he always gets hard for me again. Then he plunders me for everything I'm worth, murmuring how much he loves me in my ear.

How many memories we'll make together. How wonderful of a life we'll have.

Zan grows quickly, and after only six months, he's developed enough razor-sharp little teeth that he can eat the meat that Zakarion brings back from his hunts. Thank goodness, because I couldn't take feeding him myself anymore. He comes with me now on my adventures, perched on my shoulder as we explore everything the natural world has to offer us.

My friends have particularly taken to the baby, holding him in their arms like a wriggly cat. Sometimes he gets feisty and bites, until Zakarion scolds him. Then Zan flattens his wings and pouts, but soon learns to keep his teeth to himself.

When he's a year old, he's grown too big for me to carry on my own. Now he hikes alongside me, his little legs trying to keep up with mine. By a year and a half, he's started babbling, and I try to teach him sign language to help him communicate with us. He takes well to it, and I find my toddler dragon has many demands to make.

By the time he's two, I've finally forgotten enough about the day Zan was born to consider another one.

Zakarion raises his brows when I tell him that I'm pondering it.

"I didn't think you'd want that," he says, voice tinged with hopefulness. "But I will happily seed you with many, many hatchlings."

"Well, let's start at two." I giggle. "They're quite a lot to handle. Then we can talk about more."

On the night of the full moon, we put Zan to bed, and then my dragon carries me up into the sky. There, bathed in ethereal light, he plunges inside me, both of us crying our pleasure into the night. He fills me thoroughly, until he's dripping out of me from this great height, and slowly he brings us back to earth.

We make memory after memory, and it isn't long before we're pregnant with another hatchling.

One night, after Zakarion finishes reading from the notebook to Zan, we curl up in our nest with a new life growing inside me.

"I love you," I tell my dragon, wrapping my arms around his long neck. I don't know how much time we have together, and neither does he—but we will treasure every last moment of it.

He bends his head down to hook his chin over my shoulder. "Sammy," he murmurs, stroking my back with his claws. "I don't even think 'love' describes how I feel about you."

I scoff. "Always have to outdo me."

He chuckles and draws me into his warm chest, his fire radiating from inside.

Zakarion

My life with Sammy is far more magical, filled with laughter and love and desire, than I could have ever dreamed. I share everything with our hatchlings: the story of my long life and all the lives that came before me, of all the treasures we acquired and then sent home to where they belong. Zan becomes a marvelous adult, and is soon old enough to venture out on his own and discover everything the world holds for him—something I never did. He is curious about all the marvelous places represented in our stories, and pledges to learn everything he can. He will find other dragons, and seek to preserve our history.

It is hard for us to let him go, but we have given him every tool possible, and we have to believe that he'll thrive.

Time slows as our hatchlings grow up and then move out one by one, and the mountain becomes quiet again. I never could have imagined a life so full for myself, and as twilight falls, I am grateful for its shade.

Every night, I hold my Sammy in my arms, and tell her just how much she means to me—how she is my everything.

THANK YOU SO MUCH FOR READING!

If you enjoyed Sammy and Zakarion's story, please consider leaving a review! Reviews are incredibly helpful to indie authors like me in reaching new readers.

join my newsletter!

For all the latest, and to get access to a FREE novella, join my newsletter! You can also buy paperback copies and prints of your favorite books.

www.LyonneRiley.com

I come from a traditional publishing background, which is rewarding but often too rigid, so I shifted to self-publishing to pursue my real passion in writing: extremely sexy non-human romance. I probably should have known I would end up here after spending most of my young adulthood writing erotic fan fiction, but it took me a while to find my way back to myself.

acknowledgments

I would like to thank everyone involved in helping me through the process of putting out this book. I can't say enough how much I appreciate the help and encouragement of the people around me—especially Amber, who told me I could do this in the first place.

Huge thank you to Rowan Woodcock for the gorgeous cover illustration. To my critique partners, who gave me phenomenal feedback: You all make this possible. And of course, my amazing spouse, who has always supported my dreams—and given me lots of inspiration for my characters' sexy adventures.

I couldn't have done this without the expertise of my fellow self-published romance authors. Thank you for inviting me into your circles and helping me through this process.

And thank you to my readers, who gave this book a shot.